THE
STONE BABY

Also by the same author

THE VESPUCCI PAPERS
WAITING FOR A TIGER
THE TERRIBLE PICTURES

THE
STONE BABY

By

BEN HEALEY

J. B. LIPPINCOTT COMPANY
Philadelphia and New York

U.S. Library of Congress Cataloging in Publication Data

Healey, Ben.
    The stone baby.

    I. Title.
PZ4.H4343St   [PR6058.E17]   823'.9'14   73–667
ISBN–0–397–00957–7

C ./

All of the characters in this book are fictitious except Alceo Dossena and, of course, Michelangelo.

There is very little recent work on the life of Dossena but the main facts of his curious career in Rome of the nineteen twenties, as given by Harcourt d'Espinal, are substantially correct so far as can be known. He represents probably one of the greatest personal enigmas in the history of art—whether he was merely a persistent forger or an exceptionally innocent genius—and, although we have no record that he ever did carve a Sleeping Cupid, there is very little doubt that, judging by the standards of his recognized works, he would have found no difficulty in doing so.

Of the several versions of the Sleeping Cupid story, that again given by d'Espinal is probably the most accurate: it was originally sold as a forgery and it did disappear about 1631. It is interesting also that Michelangelo carved a second cupid a year or so later, in 1497, for Jacopo Galli, a Roman banker of that period. This was described as the Cupid Awakening, and this too has vanished.

Chapter One

Bruno Cavalli said simply, "I am afraid."

It was quiet in the small room, and shadowy in spite of the heat and glare of midmorning sunlight outside, so that the pictures hanging on paneled walls seemed to glow softly in a greenish-tinted light from the window: two arches divided by a slender spiral pillar and streaky glass which distorted the carved decoration of the building across the canal. Greenish like the water below, and faintly tremulous from the reflected ripple patterns flickering and chasing each other endlessly across the ceiling. Wherever you went in this damned Venice you saw those reflections, Bruno Cavalli thought. He had no mind for them; they were as restless as the city itself and they worried him, as this whole affair was worrying him.

Sitting each side of an antique desk, the two men were almost ludicrously dissimilar. Cavalli small and plump, sweating slightly in his summer suit of a rather unpleasant light-brown color; the other casually dressed in linen trousers and a silk shirt, yet somehow still looking as if he were in the discipline of uniform. Cavalli a round, even apparently childish face except for the calculating eyes and a hint of angry obstinacy about the mouth; Colonel Mark Raven, leaning back in a brocaded chair and silhouetted against the window, bleak and gray and watchful. He shifted slightly, impatiently, and repeated, "You are afraid. Of what?"

Cavalli's voice was spiteful. "What is your English expression? We are out of our depth."

"I'm not," Raven corrected him gently. "You may be. I find it surprising. Sabbioni said nobody could handle the Cupid better."

"Sabbioni . . ." It was almost an expletive. "Sabbioni grows more malignant as he grows older. He is merely amusing himself with one last deal before he dies. And that is long overdue."

"Sabbioni's terms were that you should take a third of any final settlement. As we stand at present, roughly three hundred and thirty thousand dollars. I don't find that amusing. Or malignant."

"It will be screamingly amusing if I am dead too." Cavalli leaned forward suddenly, spreading out both hands palm upwards on the desk. "Answer me one question, Colonel Raven. Icarus Polliano pretends he will pay one million dollars. But why?" Without waiting for an answer, he went on, "Polliano is a barbarian, a brute." He stopped suddenly and then said more quietly, "I never enter a matter of this kind without making the most careful inquiries."

"You've mentioned this before, several times. Polliano has an ugly reputation. But I imagine his money is still good enough."

"Polliano is an *assassino*." Cavalli used the Italian word, screwing up his eyes fretfully, thinking that this colonel too was a barbarian. All the English were barbarians—they must be, or they would not be English. "I will tell you again. Extortion, murder—or murder by his orders—beatings, drug trafficking. Dear God, it should be enough for one man's life-time."

Raven sighed faintly. "And three years ago he decided it was. He left New York in a hurry and prudently retired from active business."

The hint of bleak humor seemed to infuriate Cavalli. "Does that kind ever retire? It is true that he now resides on a small villa estate near Rome with his two remaining men, if one may call them such. But that does not suddenly make him a saint."

"I don't understand," Raven complained. "If you're so afraid of this man, why did you ever take the deal on?"

Cavalli slapped the desk with the palm of his hand. "Because I did not know. Old Sabbioni called me in Milan. He told me only that we had a nice little business here, that you wished to sell the Cupid and he had found a purchaser. It remained only for me to complete the matter and get the best price possible. I did not know it was Polliano."

Raven watched him dispassionately. Tortuous minds, he thought, both Sabbioni and this man. The Roman mania for intrigue. It was extraordinary: give almost any Roman the choice between a simple deal with profit at the end of it and a complicated chess game of move and countermove, and he would choose the game instinctively. It was in the blood.

"So I made my inquiries," Cavalli was saying. "Polliano is worth a little over two million dollars, American. He is a Sicilian. He is, or he claims to be, a sick man, and according to his lawyer's secretary—dear God, that woman cost me over two hundred thousand lire in one night—when he passes on, this money will go to the lawyer himself and Polliano's two men. Riccardo Castello, a Corsican, and Alberto Mazzoni, another Sicilian." Cavalli leaned forward, again slapping his hand on the desk. "Colonel Raven, is it rational that a creature of such type should be prepared to spend one half of his entire fortune on a piece of sculpture, not even a very large piece?"

"It's curious, certainly," the colonel admitted.

"Curious?" Cavalli breathed. "The English affectation of understatement. It is fantasy. I have a great deal of experience, Colonel. You will recollect that Polliano started by offering two hundred and fifty thousand, and then raised it to five hundred. That is where we should have settled." He stabbed his forefinger at Raven accusingly. "But you yourself, when he came on to seven fifty, demanded we should hold for a million. It is not good sense. Polliano will not pay one million dollars; he does not intend to. Therefore he will make his own methods. Murder—or beating."

Again it was the curious passion for intrigue, Raven thought, melodrama. Never once had Cavalli approached Polliano openly; all the negotiations so far had been by letter or telephone. The little man had insisted this was the best way in the early stages, the most discreet, and Raven himself had not troubled to interfere. He said ironically, "I see the reason for your odd methods. You seem to imagine the man's Satan in person."

"It would be much simpler if he were. Any competent village priest could deal with the devil, but the Holy Father himself might think twice about two Sicilians and a Corsican." Cavalli grinned mirthlessly, as if deciding that was not such a good joke after all. "Let us face it, there will come a time when I must produce the Cupid. And what happens then?" He drew a forefinger across his throat and made an unpleasant guttural sound. "No Cupid, no one million dollars, no Bruno Cavalli any more. That is how Polliano works, and I have a very natural objection." He paused for a long half minute, watching Raven, and then went on: "Let us be realistic. Better still, let us talk business. There is another possibility, a safe one. I have heard of an American, a most charming, cultured person, who arrives in Venice shortly. A curator of one of the great museums."

"There'd be too much publicity. I want it settled quietly."

"We can start at three hundred thousand and I might perhaps bring him up to four hundred or even five."

"No," Raven interrupted flatly. There was another silence while he reached forward and minutely adjusted the position of an elegant little antique silver clock on the desk. He said, "Signor Cavalli, I have seen this coming for some time, and you cannot blame me if I make my own arrangements. If I appoint another agent."

"If you what?" Cavalli whispered. He stared at

Raven incredulously. "Do I understand that you discharge me?"

"Wouldn't it be better to say you decided to withdraw?"

"I see." Cavalli's voice was toneless. "And Sabbioni?"

"He will receive his third share when the deal is settled. And yourself your expenses, with a quite generous appreciation for your time and trouble."

"I see," Cavalli repeated. He screwed up his eyes to peer at Raven against the greenish window. "And who is . . . this agent?"

"His name is d'Espinal. Harcourt d'Espinal. In fact I am meeting him this morning."

"I see," Cavalli said once more. He appeared to think about that for some time too, and then with both hands on the edge of the desk he slowly pushed himself upright, asking, "Who is this Harcourt d'Espinal?" But before Raven could tell him he exploded, "It does not matter. I shall find out. You do realize that this is a damned insult? And you realize that I still hold the Cupid?"

"As I hold the documents proving it to be a Michelangelo. Without those you cannot sell the Cupid. And without the Cupid they are so much wastepaper." The bleak smile appeared. "It looks like a stalemate. Come now, Cavalli, you must see that we're tied up together. Why not let d'Espinal do the work for us? And take the risks, if there are any. When you've had time to work it out you'll be willing to agree."

Cavalli was already halfway out of the room, but he

stopped with one hand on the door, looking back over his shoulder. Stammering slightly, he said, "You cannot do it, Colonel. The Cupid could so easily be lost again."

Mr. Harcourt d'Espinal stepped ashore from his boat opposite the rose-pink walls and arcades of the Ducal Palace, the sunlight making an impressionist picture of broken color and movement in the crowds on the white marble pavement. A master painter's rendering of the water under the ferryboats and motor launches and black gondolas fussing at the landing stages; malachite green breaking into sapphire, passing into pearl and gold, and the distant shimmer of the Lido across the lagoon, the particular Venetian quality of light like blue champagne, he thought fancifully. He beamed down at his boatman and said, "Do not trouble to wait, Pietro, old friend; I will have a taxi bring me back to San Giorgio Piccolo in time for tea."

At this moment he had no presentiment of danger, except perhaps that with almost as nice a sense of words as he had of pictures he did not care for the colonel's name; it was, he considered, devilishly ill-omened. But his invitation to call at the house on the Calle della Pietà had been more than courteous, and the hint that they might both find the meeting mutually profitable still more promising. So walking majestically along the waterfront, rather like an amiable Roman emperor in a dove-gray London-cut suiting, Mr. d'Espinal allowed his mind to dwell pleasantly on Emilia Pentecost's latest achievement—a trifle, but a delightful trifle. The dear girl was rapidly developing what had merely been latent talent into something like pure genius for forgery, this time a study of cats by Jacopo Bassano, that fine old painter of the High Renaissance who would introduce animals into a Last Supper or into an Adoration of the Shepherds on the lightest of excuses. If the good colonel was seriously thinking in terms of mutual profit, one certainly might do worse than mention dear Emilia's little Bassano—with the nicest diplomacy, of course.

D'Espinal's entire existence, indeed, was a matter of nice diplomacy. With his apartment in London overlooking Richmond Park and a second home here in Venice on the private island of San Giorgio Piccolo—where Mrs. Judith Teestock presided most admirably and her niece and companion, Emilia, produced such perfectly executed new works by old masters—it needed the very nicest to preserve all of these delightful things from any touch of scandal, perhaps even of the law. However civilized and urbane, the life of a dealer in forged works of art was a tricky, precarious business. Like the Bridge of Sighs, spanning this canal between the palace and the Old Prison, the passage between a glowing vista of life and light and movement and the darkness of a penitential limbo could be a short and sudden one.

But for the present you had the spectacle of Venice in early September in all its infinite variety. A party of brightly dressed girls drifting past like butterflies and laughing back at him as he smiled benevolently on them. The glimpse of a small boy with an impudent grin. News vendors and flower sellers; two municipal guardsmen parading in gleaming white uniforms, each with one hand resting elegantly on his sword hilt. And then suddenly the child, appearing out of the shade by the Danieli Hotel, curiously alone in the crowd, whispering, "Signore . . ." and looking up at him appraisingly out of a solemn little face.

It was a small girl. At first sight the cropped dark hair and wide mouth, the faded pink shirt and blue jeans looked entirely male; but the surprisingly blue Venetian eyes and the hint of cajolery in them were as feminine as Eve. And she was unmistakably a beggar—distressingly thin and small, although, he judged, perhaps as much as twelve years old. She held out a fan of gaudy picture postcards and said, "Signore, by your favor, all views of Venice."

D'Espinal gazed down. He murmured, "Come now, my dear. I am in this trade myself. Would you sell to a fellow dealer?"

That seemed to puzzle her, but she recognized the kindliness in his voice clearly enough, and the corners of her lips went down, the Venetian eyes slanted up at him sideways. "So perhaps you need a guide. I know all of Venice."

"Nor do I really need a guide," d'Espinal answered. The corners of her mouth drooped a little more and the eyes, he imagined, looked defeated. He murmured, "Poor child," and felt in his pocket to produce a hundred-lire piece, saying, "While you almost certainly need ice cream or chocolate, or some such frivolity. What is your name?"

She said, "Angela Caterina. And a thousand thanks, signore. I shall buy pizza; there is more body in that." Her eyes moved past him nervously; she was poised to run, but still paused long enough to repeat, "A thousand thanks."

D'Espinal himself glanced back too. The municipal guards—no longer the merely decorative figures they had seemed only a few minutes ago—had turned and were watching the girl; you could see that they did not like beggars, and the child herself was openly afraid of them. D'Espinal nodded. "I understand your position. Very well, then, to avoid any slight trouble with the guards you shall guide me as far as the Calle della Pietà."

She flashed a wide grin of conspiracy up at him. "Signore, you are very kind. One day I will light a candle for you in San Marco—when I have the money to buy a candle."

"And I have no doubt," he said, "that in Heaven a candle from a child will be more effective than the blessing of a bishop. Let us move on then, Angela Caterina. Those gentlemen in white are still watching you."

Colonel Raven was now standing with his back to the window, so that again he was little more than a silhouette against the wavering light behind. When the woman showed d'Espinal in, his own first impression was of warning, in spite of the fine antique furniture and the quiet comfort of the room; he felt that, even apart from the fellow's ominous name, mutual advantage with Colonel Raven could perhaps be a somewhat one-sided affair, and that it might be wise to tread cautiously until one knew what he wanted. But then the colonel came forward to the desk holding out his hand and saying, "Mr. d'Espinal, it's very good of you to call, and at such short notice. I know you're a busy man." The thin, straight lips were relieved by a smile of sudden, surprising charm, and he added, "It's uncommonly good of you, and I'm obliged. But sit down, please. A glass of wine?"

There was a long-necked bottle swathed in a napkin and two Venetian goblets on a silver tray, and Raven poured the pale liquid carefully, murmuring, "The Niersteiner Eiswein. A little eccentric to drink it at this hour, perhaps."

"Sir," d'Espinal announced, "it cannot be counted eccentric to drink such wine at any hour." He tasted it delicately and breathed, "Exquisite."

The colonel's look of unaffected pleasure seemed to suggest that he had been waiting only to hear that word. "Sixty-two," he explained. "As you will know, the autumn in Germany was ideal for it that year. Dry and frosty right on into November." He savored his own glass carefully, holding it up to the light to catch the lambent glint of sunshine in it, and said, "One knows your reputation, Mr. d'Espinal." Only the closest observation could have seen d'Espinal stiffen slightly, watching the other man, thinking grimly that it all depended upon which reputation. And almost as if he had picked up the thought, Raven went on, "As an expert on Renaissance art, an authority."

D'Espinal's eyelids drooped lower. "A mere salesman, sir. But one tries to be scholarly."

"And with success, with unique success. That's why I must not waste your time."

The man was too fulsome, d'Espinal told himself

darkly. It was almost naïve, and naïveté and Colonel Raven clearly were somewhat improbable bedfellows. And was there perhaps a hint, the very slightest hint, of threat? Time no doubt would show, but for the present it might be as well to forget Emilia's latest little offering and affect innocence oneself. He said modestly, "You're too kind, sir."

"Far from it," Raven insisted, and that at least was probably correct. "The fact is that I'm concerned in a rather delicate business. And it needs an expert." D'Espinal somehow contrived to look even more modest, and Raven explained, "I was at one of Mrs. Messina-Silvestro's tea parties a few days ago."

Wondering whether that again was a hint of threat, d'Espinal agreed, "They are a chastening experience. I am sometimes bidden to them myself."

"Your name was mentioned, and I thought, That's the man I need, if I can get him interested. I hope I can." Raven stopped and then finished, "Let me show you something."

Reaching down to the side of his chair he brought up a small wooden box, holding it in both hands for a moment before placing it on the desk and taking out something white—strangely and horribly like a death mask—and d'Espinal jerked his eyes wide open suddenly, staring distastefully for a moment before leaning forward to examine it more closely. A baby's head in plaster: the eyes closed, on the lips a faint smile which was at once childish and wanton, and somehow expressed in the modeling was a hint of ancient mischievous knowledge far beyond its apparent years. It was no human baby. It was a cast, apparently from some piece of sculpture, and whatever the original might have been, d'Espinal thought, it was certainly the work of a master—and from the style and manner, a Renaissance master.

"Do you recognize it?" Raven asked.

D'Espinal looked up at him from under his eyelids. "I have no authority in sculpture. I am, as it were, a man of paint. The original, I would say, is dated about 1490 to 1500. And it is not unlike the Child of the Bruges Madonna. But that is Michelangelo."

"So is this," Raven said. "It is the Sleeping Cupid."

D'Espinal sighed faintly. He had pulled too many confidence tricks himself not to know another when he saw it—and one so singularly inept, so flatly impossible. Half closing his eyes once more, he murmured, "No, Colonel Raven. I can take a miracle as well as the next man. I positively enjoy a good miracle. But not this one. The Sleeping Cupid of Michelangelo disappeared in 1631. It has never been seen since."

"And where is it now?"

"Does it even exist now? If it does, and since it is last recorded as being purchased from the d'Este family on behalf of King Charles the First of England, I would guess that it might be somewhere in Windsor Castle. If it ever reached England."

Raven said, "It did not reach England. Suppose I told you that the Sleeping Cupid is here now, in Venice?"

"Regretfully, sir, most regretfully, I should say you were indulging in fantasy."

The colonel laughed. "I don't think so. Let me show you these too." This time he opened a drawer in the desk and took out a manila folder, enlarged photographs, perhaps half a dozen or more sheets of photocopy paper.

D'Espinal was examining the cast again minutely; his eyes narrowed. "Pray tell me," he asked, "how did you come by this?"

"It's a long story." Raven pushed the photographs and papers across his desk. "Perhaps you'd care to look at these."

Glancing at him briefly, d'Espinal took them without speaking. The photographs were all of the Cupid, taken from varying angles and with enlarged details —highly professional pictures which revealed even the patina and the stains of apparently rougher weathering. A sleeping child, its right hand under its head, lying on its back in a relaxed pose with the legs slightly apart. Exactly as the Cupid was described somewhere, in some contemporary reference. D'Espinal brooded over that for a moment before he placed it. The Inventory of Mantua.

He examined the pictures one by one in silence, his face expressionless, and no trace now of his habitual mannerisms; he was an expert, a businessman considering something which all his knowledge and reason told him must be a hoax, and a hoax, moreover, in which apparently he was somehow to be involved. Stacking the photographs to the side deliberately, making a little rattling noise with them on the desk, he laid out the other papers without looking at Raven. These were photostat copies of documents, four of them typed, others written in several hands, all in Italian, and some so crabbed or faded as to be almost unreadable, all signed with different signatures, but all countersigned "Niccolò Sabbioni" and—under the countersign—dated less than six months before. He studied these for a moment too and then asked, "Niccolò Sabbioni of the Via Veneto, Rome?"

"His name should be good enough," Raven said.

D'Espinal looked up again, wondering curiously how much Raven really knew about that old rascal, and then agreed, "Indeed it should; none better."

He turned back to the papers, reading from one: " 'Consistent in all details with an item listed as the Sleeping Cupid of Michelangelo in the "Collection of Isabella d'Este," ' et cetera," turning over the other typewritten sheets and murmuring, "Chemical, X-ray and microscopic examination. We may take it they will be unimpeachable; Sabbioni has always been very thorough." The hand-written documents appeared to interest him more and he considered these, pouting slightly, turning back from one to another, and at last asking, "Garzeno. Where is that? And this Domenico Galli?"

"A farmer, a very old man," Raven told him shortly. "Garzeno is near Lake Como. Mr. d'Espinal, if you're interested you can take those papers. They're only copies."

"Yes," d'Espinal murmured, "I am indeed interested —I'm fascinated." He appeared to brood heavily before asking, "What exactly do you want of me?"

"To negotiate the sale." The charming smile appeared once more. "I'll be frank with you. It's a curious position, but my title to the Cupid is sound. You'll find a receipt there by Domenico Galli for half a million lire—just over three hundred pounds, or nearly eight hundred dollars."

"I already have. Not a very large sum for a Michelangelo, surely?"

"At that time I did not know it was a Michelangelo. It was merely a small figure found in a stable. May I go on? It was sent to Sabbioni for expert examination. And he announced that it could only be the Sleeping Cupid and asked me if I was interested in selling. What do you think I said, Mr. d'Espinal? I'm not a collector, nor even a particularly wealthy man. And it appears that he already had a prospective purchaser. But he made certain conditions."

"Niccolò Sabbioni would, of course. What were they?"

"One, that it should be handled by his own agent, which seemed reasonable enough. Two, that in consideration of further research to establish what they tell me is called the provenance and attestations—those papers—he, the agent, and myself should take equal shares of the figure ultimately realized. I felt that was too much, but I want to sell the thing and can't do it alone. And to these the agent added one more. That he should hold the Cupid while in turn I retained the documents which prove its authenticity. So we can't move without each other. Quite simply I thought this was just typical of the eternal damned Roman mania for intrigue."

It was typical, d'Espinal thought, of three people who did not trust each other an inch. He said, "I've heard of similar arrangements. The third share is extortionate perhaps, but even that . . . "—he chuckled softly, looking again at the smiling head on the desk between them—". . . even that is part of the history of this pretty child. When Michelangelo sold the work originally in 1496 he did so through the agency of one Baldassare di Milanese. And Baldassare took two hundred gold florins for it but only paid Michelangelo thirty."

The colonel did not appear to be interested in history. He asked, "Mr. d'Espinal, will you take this business over?"

D'Espinal looked thoughtful. "I'll confess my interest. But there are difficulties. Even among art dealers dog does not eat dog—or not more than a hind leg or two. Sabbioni and his present agent may not offer me the kindest of welcomes."

"I can attend to that. The Cupid is my property."

Finishing his glass of wine, d'Espinal allowed the colonel to refill it, blandly watching the ripple reflections at their endless dance across the ceiling, before he murmured, "There's a doubt, you know. The Italian State might demand it. Or even the Crown of England on a claim that the d'Este family did indeed sell it to Charles the First. What a field day these lawyer fellows would make of it." He smiled gently at Raven. "I take it you've thought of that? So I imagine you'd wish the sale to be effected with some discretion, as it were."

"The sale's already arranged. With an Italian-American named Icarus Polliano, staying at the Hotel Ludovico Manin on the Lido. He's prepared to pay one million dollars."

The eyelids lifted a little. "It seems a neat, simple sum. What is your difficulty?"

"Simply, the damn fool I'm saddled with does not

like Polliano. He wants to offer the Cupid elsewhere at a lower price."

"Dear me," d'Espinal breathed, "with a million dollars at stake, that smacks of a niceness which borders on eccentricity. Why?"

Raven hesitated. There were several things it was best not to tell d'Espinal for the present, especially Polliano's reputation and who Sabbioni's agent was; one might frighten him off before he was committed, the other lead to still more intrigue. He said, "He seems to think Polliano's credit may be dubious."

"Dear me." D'Espinal sounded slightly shocked. "What very odd people there are in the world—even a little dishonest sometimes. I take it you're not tied to this Polliano? One is merely thinking aloud, you understand, but I have certain openings too—a small consortium, as it were. We might buy for an investment . . . I don't know," he murmured. "I should like to consider it for a day or two. And of course I must examine the Cupid for myself."

"Of course," Raven agreed. That need not be difficult; Cavalli could be forced to return the Cupid easily enough when necessary. "But don't consider it for too long, Mr. d'Espinal. A million dollars might not wait, and I'm not seriously interested in less."

"Why should you be?" d'Espinal asked. He was faintly amused. What an unwise colonel it was.

Carrying the colonel's folder of pictures and photostats, d'Espinal emerged from the narrow quietness of the Calle della Pietà into the wide light and glitter of the waterfront again. A most useful and instructive morning, he considered, though perhaps a pity that one would have to forget dear Emilia's little Bassano for a time in favor of the far bigger prize; but a million dollars was not to be sneezed at lightly. Turning out along the Riva Schiavoni, more like an amiable Roman emperor than ever, he repeated that it had been a most promising morning indeed. He did not notice the other man, the angry, insulted face fifty yards or so behind him, and would not have recognized him if he had.

Neither did Bruno Cavalli, sick with his own rage, see the small girl slipping along so unobtrusively after him in turn; nobody ever does see beggars until they become importunate. D'Espinal moving irresistably through the crowds; Cavalli cursing his own impotence, telling himself that one must be subtle, that there was too much at stake to go at this damned Englishman like a mad bull; Angela Caterina working out in her curious little mind that there was something very strange when one signore trailed another like this, muttering and whispering to himself—which everybody knew was talking to the devil and could even cause a death. Thinking too that if she herself told the big signore about it, perhaps he would give her another hundred lire.

They went on, one after the other, until d'Espinal came abreast of the glass doors of the Hotel Danieli and paused there, apparently undecided whether to go in or not. In that short time Cavalli himself quickened his pace. But then d'Espinal moved on again towards the wide marble bridge over the Palazzo Canal; the shady side of San Marco, he felt—Florian's—was the best place to take an aperitif today. He was to reflect afterwards in his rococo manner that on such fragile chances hang the threads of life. Had he turned into the Danieli, Cavalli would have followed him, while the child would certainly not have been admitted and he might never have seen her again.

Chapter Two

It was probably the waiter who really made everything inevitable, flapping his napkin at the child and
snarling. While d'Espinal sat watching the drifting,
chattering spectacle of what he personally considered
to be the most beautiful city square in the world—the
elegant, sunlit façades, the colored and gilded cathedral
like a page from an illuminated manuscript—she came
picking her way between the tables at Florian's like a
small, nervous cat at a banquet. He might have been
satisfied just to give her another hundred lire and send
her packing himself. But when Stefano hissed, "Be
off there, miserable beggar," and she flinched back,
the child's appeal touched d'Espinal—appeal and
an unexpected hint of determination in the wide, blue
eyes. He said sharply, "Stop, Stefano. That will do."

The waiter stared at him. He started, "It is out of all
order—" but again the ugly, hungry little face touched
d'Espinal and he interrupted firmly, "You may bring
her ice cream. Or something more substantial. She
is partial to pizza, I believe."

"Pizza?" Stefano breathed incredulously. "At
Florian's?"

"What you will, then," d'Espinal told him testily.
"But food. The child is hungry." Stefano took a deep
breath, but d'Espinal's face was forbidding suddenly,
and he shrugged and turned away; if your patrons

chose to go mad it was their own affair, and this one always paid generously. "He knows me," d'Espinal explained, but then shook his head severely at Angela, now half sitting on the edge of a chair, still clutching her forlorn little fan of picture postcards. "All the same, you must not follow people. You really mustn't. It could lead to an embarrassment."

"But, signore," she whispered, "I only followed the signore because some other person also was following him."

D'Espinal blinked at her. "Following me?"

She nodded vigorously. "He is there now, at a table in front. A small man but nearly as fat as you are."

"Fat?" demanded d'Espinal awfully.

He was sorry at once. The child flinched again at his voice. "I am sorry, signore. Not so imposing. With the *cappuccino*-colored suit and white hat. He is now looking over his shoulder at you."

"How extraordinary," d'Espinal murmured. But it was quite true; there was a person wearing a light milky-brown suit, now turning his head away again furtively, and apparently speaking to someone d'Espinal could not see.

Angela said, "There is another man. Signor Light Brown stopped and spoke to this one as if he knew him, and then sat down at the same table. He is out of your sight from here because of that large pink lady with the wide hat. But he is a little man with a sharp nose, like a . . ."—she searched for the word—"*pappagallo*. The bird that bites."

"Parrot," d'Espinal suggested, and then said, "Dear me." So far as he knew there was only one man in

Venice who might fit that description, and he moved sideways for a clearer view. "Dear me," he repeated distastefully, surveying the crested yellowish-gray hair, the beaked nose and curious sidling, sideways movements. "Venturi. That vexatious nuisance."

Again he was to think afterwards that it was another coincidence. Had he not so clearly shown his own dislike of this spiteful little man—Emilia, indeed, detested the creature—the child herself might have lost interest. As it was, she clearly scented an exciting mystery. She whispered, "Signore, is he a bad man?"

"My dear," d'Espinal asked, "what is a bad man? Do you know? Let us say he is not a nice one."

Angela had no time for subtleties. She announced firmly, "They are both bad men. You may not know, signore, being English, but when people talk to themselves like that one did it is very bad luck. It could even mean that someone will die."

"Now, child," d'Espinal protested, "this really is nonsense."

"I considered you should be told," she went on. "When you went into that house on the calle I myself sat on a bridge over the canal thinking how best to spend your hundred lire. Also I thought if I waited you might wish to go to some other place and perhaps give me another hundred."

"I see you are a businesswoman."

"One does not get very much pizza for only that much. Well, then I saw this other signore. He was standing under an archway looking at that house, and I watched him too. Then when you came out again he followed you down the calle and out to the

Schiavoni and all the way here. And when we came by the Church of the Pietà he was cursing. It is particularly bad to curse outside a church."

D'Espinal was amused. "Rather worse inside, one would think." Angela considered that seriously for a moment, but Stefano came back then, announcing "*Ecco,*" inquiring sardonically, "Will that be sufficient, do you think?" and she whispered, "Oh, signore."

"Chicken livers and savory meatballs," Stefano said. "With Coca-Cola. And *gelati* to follow. She will be sick, of course," he observed dispassionately.

For the next few minutes d'Espinal could do little but watch with a sort of distressed fascination, forgetting about the odd fellow in brown and murmuring, "When did you last eat? You must not go at it so fast, child." When at last she sat back and sighed, he asked, "Now Angela Caterina, what is your other name and where do you come from?"

The solemn little face, now slightly greasy about the lips, became secretive suddenly. "I live in Venice."

"But, my dear child," he said, "how do you live?"

"I do very well," she told him. "Not always as well as this, but enough."

"Where do you sleep?"

"Many places. There is a nice shed in the Exposition Gardens. Or now and again under the end of the Accademia Bridge, but one has to be careful of the police there. And I know a man named Mario who works a boat from the markets. That has a cover on it, but you have to get up very early in the morning. Then there is a café-bar where sometimes they let me carry things and wash dishes. It seems to me," she told him severely, "that you would do better to think about that man who is following you."

"My poor child," he said. But of course the answer was very simple, he thought. The answer was Judith Teestock. Send the girl to San Giorgio Piccolo where, in spite of their other somewhat illegal activities, the admirable Judith devoted the greater part of her life to good works; she would handle this calmly and firmly. He asked, "How would you like it if I sent you to a very kind and generous lady?"

Angela looked at him suspiciously. The woman at the café-bar was kind too sometimes, but she had once heard her saying, "We ought to take that girl to the police. She'll come to no good like this."

"This lady would look after you," d'Espinal coaxed. "Perhaps find out where your home is."

She stared at him briefly and then slid off the chair. "You are very kind, signore, and that was beautiful food. I shall never forget it. But I must go now."

Looking at her helplessly, d'Espinal realized too late that somehow he had made a mistake, but at that moment Stefano returned with the ice cream, and Angela stared at the improbable confection with wide eyes, whispering, "For me?" She glanced at d'Espinal once more but then sat down again quickly. *Gelati* like that was worth almost any risk.

D'Espinal was feeling in his inside pocket, taking out a visiting card. He said, "Now, Angela, here is my name, you see?" She disengaged herself from the ice cream just long enough to nod politely, and he went on, "I am going to write down the lady's name. 'Mrs. Judith Teestock, Isola San Giorgio Piccolo.' And the telephone number. I want you to keep this very carefully. And then if you find you need help you may go there. Do you understand?" He found a few coins, about a thousand lire, and finished, "This will help you a little. And you must think about that kind lady."

Sighing gently again for such beautiful ice cream, especially the walnuts and cherries embedded in it, Angela promised, "I will. Indeed I will. I will think about almost anything for *gelati* like that and so much money. And if there was something else I could do now?" She looked past d'Espinal at the other table and whispered, "He is still there, signore. If I were to follow him when he leaves, as he followed you—to see where he goes? I could do that very well."

D'Espinal was startled. The prospect of this solemn child dogging a probably perfectly respectable citizen all over Venice was really quite alarming. He said, "Most certainly not. You'll get yourself into fearful trouble. You must do no such thing."

"No?" Angela murmured. She seemed disappointed, eyeing him sideways, edging off the chair, and then saying darkly, "You should be very careful, signore. To my mind no good can come of this."

She slipped away, watching two of the municipal guardsmen again, and disappeared like an eel, while d'Espinal looked down at Colonel Raven's folder for a moment, brooding ponderously on the strangeness of values when you had one child made of stone, which someone seemed to think was worth a million dollars, and another—breathing and living and desperately in need of help—who appeared to have no value at all. The bright spectacle of Saint Mark's Square seemed to have lost some of its glitter—the darker side of Venice starting to show through. Unaccountably he felt the first vague touch of foreboding, as if that child with her strange, wise innocence was somehow fateful, and he told himself fretfully, Really, my dear fellow, you must not give way to these graveyard fancies. It was all quite simple. One had other friends here. He would tell them to look out for the girl, and for the rest, her story of that fellow in the unpleasant brown suit, now talking so earnestly to Venturi, was almost certainly little more than a pathetic fantasy.

So far, at least, Angela was right. Cavalli did know Venturi, as he made it his business to know many people in the antique art world of Rome, Milan and here. Professor Venturi, one time of the Accademia, one time a critic and, Cavalli considered, not a particularly reliable expert. A disappointed and spiteful man with a nose for malicious gossip, but now just at this time and place perhaps very useful. As Angela had noticed, Cavalli had stopped at his table holding out his hands, saying effusively, "Ecco, my dear professor. How very good, how excellent to see you." It had cost him a glass of Vecchia Romagna, which was damnably expensive at this place, and it would probably be two before the end; but after a suitable exchange of compliments and inquiries he said quietly, "Signor professor, if you look carefully now, that large person in the gray suit back near the arcade. Are you acquainted with him? His name is d'Espinal."

Cavalli loved intrigue for its own sake but, not an unkindly man himself, he was surprised and even slightly shocked by the flood of venom. "That one?" Venturi hissed. "A rogue, signore. What is worse, a charlatan. I could tell you much about that viper."

He talked fast and angrily, while Cavalli sat watching the strolling crowds and flights of pigeons, swirling the ice around in his own drink, wondering if what he would get from Venturi was worth the terrible price of that brandy. One was a businessman, after all; one did not like to pay good money for mere chatter. At last he said, "It is all a little confusing. D'Espinal appeared in Venice in May of last summer, and he was brought here by these two women. That is something, but not important. And a Botticelli which you say is genuine, so it does not matter to me. Then a Ghirlandaio drawing which you say is a forgery. This might be more interesting perhaps. Let us go back," he suggested. "Who is the Signora Teestock?"

Venturi pecked into his brandy. "The padrona of this Isola San Giorgio Piccolo, out by San Francesco del Deserto. Very remote. One of these high-nosed great English ladies, or so she affects. Tweed clothes and red face, like all of them. She has been here many years, and a close friend of Mrs. Messina-Silvestro, which means everything in this place. It is said she has a passion for good works among the poor in the islands." Venturi sniggered. "And, would you believe it, she is an authority on church altar cloths. She embroiders them herself. Is not that entertaining?"

"Fascinating." Cavalli sighed faintly. "And the other? Pentecost, you say."

"A bitch," Venturi said briefly. "Younger by half than the Teestock, even handsome if you care for the cold English type. She poses as the secretary and companion but in fact is d'Espinal's accomplice, if not his mistress. That I neither know nor care. Myself, I'd as soon take a scorpion to bed. But she is a painter and a draftswoman. And she came here five, six years ago from Paris, where she contrived her living as a copyist in the Louvre. D'you see what that means?" He looked at his empty glass and peered sideways at Cavalli like an old parrot.

"It might mean anything. But most probably that she is not an original artist herself."

Venturi grunted. These Romans were all the same, all thick-headed; you could never give them a gentleman's hint, you had to drive it home with a mallet. "I always suspect that Vecchia Romagna evaporates very quickly in this heat . . . It means that she now forges drawings, cartoons, and sometimes paintings. And d'Espinal sells them."

"I would have thought that in such heat old brandy is a most unwise drink altogether. Are you sure of this? About d'Espinal?"

"I have told you, after the business of the Botticelli he took up residence on San Giorgio, and now from time to time he appears and disappears. That is mysterious in itself, my friend. Then there was the Ghirlandaio drawing which he presented to Mrs. Messina-Silvestro."

"Who is this Mrs. Messina-Silvestro? Is she important in Venice?"

"Important in Venice?" Venturi looked at him incredulously. "Good God, she *is* Venice. It is said that when Mrs. Messina-Silvestro dies the Campanile will fall down again. I hope it may not be too long delayed."

Cavalli sighed once more. "The Ghirlandaio drawing . . ." he suggested.

The professor settled down as if preparing to deliver a lecture to his students. "You will recollect that

Ghirlandaio was the young Michelangelo's first master, about 1488. And that he possessed a portfolio of studies, heads and figures, which Michelangelo stole one day and then proceeded to make certain copies which were so perfect . . . "

"Wait," Cavalli interrupted, and Venturi stared at him again, alarmed this time. The change was startling. He was leaning forward across the table looking, as Venturi thought, like murder. "Professor," he asked softly, "why do you bring in Michelangelo?"

Venturi himself drew back, bowing and sidling. "Why not? It is part of this affair. What is the matter with you?"

Cavalli took a deep breath and nodded. "Of course." He mopped his face. "A passing feeling. It is the heat. Please continue. I will call another brandy for you."

Waiting for him to signal the waiter, Venturi went on rather distrustfully, "D'Espinal presented Mrs. Messina-Silvestro with a supposed Ghirlandaio study earlier this year—as an Easter gift, he said. The stupid woman was in transports. And he was clever, you understand. It was drawn on the back of another thing, presumably by one more of the academy's apprentices, something quite worthless, and d'Espinal affected that he was not sure of it himself. It might be by the master. It might even be by Michelangelo, knowing that young rascal's gift for forgery. Or it might be by another hand altogether. It was indeed," Venturi finished bitterly. "It was by Emilia Pentecost."

"Now," the other man breathed, "we might have something. How do you know?"

Venturi struck his chest violently with a clenched fist. "I feel it here."

"Feelings of the heart do not help us very much," Cavalli said, already regretting that second brandy. "What happened to this so precious drawing by so many hands?"

"Dear God," Venturi cried, "the colossal, monumental impudence. He suggested she should offer it for sale for her Venice Restoration Fund as 'probably but perhaps dubious.'" He paused dramatically and then whispered, "It fetched seventy thousand dollars."

"In that case we may say that it was indeed a Ghirlandaio. And probably sold somewhat cheaply."

"I say it was not." The professor stabbed a stained forefinger at Cavalli. "But mark what this serpent achieved. First he secured himself a patroness for life in the Messina-Silvestro—and that is as good as a permanent seat on the state barge. Next he made certain that if the drawing ever was said to be a forgery she would deny it, since that woman can never confess she might be mistaken. And last . . ."—Venturi contrived somehow to look even more malignant—"he made me a fool."

"What is the expression?" Cavalli seemed to be unseasonably amused. "You pushed your neck out?"

"I announced it was a cheat. I proclaimed it. And what happened? That monument of a woman ordered me never to enter her house again. The serpent himself told people there comes a time when every man's eyesight begins to fail him and they should be sympathetic. And the Pentecost threatened me to bring an action at law. I would see this man dead if I could," he spat out viciously. "There was a time in Venice when one might have arranged that. But the place is soft these days."

Cavalli was visibly startled. "Let us not talk of such things," he protested quickly. "It brings ill luck." He placed some coins on the table, calculating them to the nearest five lire. "There is no more you can tell me about Signor Harcourt d'Espinal?"

"I can think of one man who must know everything." Venturi finished the second brandy and once more peered hopefully at Cavalli. "A Paolo Raffaele who has the Galleria Raffaele on the Rio della Toletta. He deals in the minor masters. A learned old fool and even said to be honest. One hears that he treats d'Espinal as his own son. Perhaps you could persuade him to talk . . ."

"If he treats the man like his son it is unlikely." Cavalli got up. The talk of seeing people dead had upset him again, and he wanted no more of this ancient, spiteful parrot. But it seemed very likely that d'Espinal really was a rogue and probably a formidable rogue, so it was time to set about making his own plans to defeat him. He said politely, "I hope we may meet again one day, Professor Venturi," and turned away across the square. Again he failed to notice the small, solemn child who detached herself from the crowd and started doggedly after him.

Paolo Raffaele was d'Espinal's oldest friend in Venice—perhaps anywhere. A dealer and collector himself, and a scholar, he lived unhurriedly in this quiet house set in a garden with old Annunzietta, his housekeeper, older-still Andreas, who pottered in the studio and gallery, and the cats, which it amused him to name after the great personalities of history: the wicked gold and silver of Cesare Borgia, Niccolò Machiavelli in black, and gray Isabella d'Este. D'Espinal he too knew was a rogue, yet he often thought that the world might be a better place if there were a few more rogues like this in it instead of many a man who imagined he was honest. It was not quite true, as Venturi said, that he treated him like a son, but there was a very real bond of tolerant, kindly affection between them, and on both sides a genuine appreciation of wide and deep learning in the other.

They were sitting with Colonel Raven's photographs and documents between them, d'Espinal brooding heavily over the golden green of the garden and the soft rose pink of a building across the canal glowing through the trees. He said, "I've only the merest embryo of a notion. But with old Sabbioni in it I smell a whiff of devilment in the air."

The elderly, quizzical face—mop of white hair and spectacles habitually askew—was mildly cynical. "With you about, it might well become more than a whiff. Let this be, Harcourt. Don't tempt fate more often than you need."

"A million dollars," d'Espinal reminded him. "And that colonel fellow's own title to the thing plainly dubious. But what is it, Paolo?"

"I don't know. But Michelangelo is too improbable." The old man reached out to the photographs, straightening his glasses to study them again. "Yet it's certainly the hand of a master. And like you, I'm inquisitive. Leave me some of these studies. Let me think about it and compare them with other pictures I have."

D'Espinal glanced across at him sharply. "You've some idea?"

"Like you again, only the merest embryo. But if I'm right . . . " He paused, looking somber suddenly. "Let it be," he repeated. "If I'm right, the man who might have carved that pretty child died half insane in a pauper hospital."

"My dear old friend," d'Espinal protested, "you spoil the afternoon." He sat with his chin sunk on his chest, eyes half closed, pouting slightly. "It's that other child who worries me, far more than this one. I was touched. She said she'd light a candle for me."

"And you have most need of it."

"Come now, Paolo," he protested again. "I've asked our Annunzietta to look out for her."

"Harcourt," Paolo said, "I am an old man. I suspect Annunzietta thinks I grow a little more foolish every year. That is the way of all good housekeepers. But if there is a thing I still know it is that you should never look out for a woman. Even a very small one of only twelve years old."

Angela Caterina was hot and tired, thirsty and a little tearful. It had been a bad afternoon. To start with she had felt very uneasy in the stomach and had later been extremely sick, although that perhaps was worth it merely to remember the beautiful ice cream and all the other food. Now she had a headache. Sitting with her feet in the water, half hidden in the grass by the side of the long white road down which the light-brown signore had vanished, she considered gravely whether that too was worth it for the sake of the other signore, the big one. One had to work these things out carefully.

He seemed to understand why she was nervous of municipal guards, although he had also said a frightening thing about finding out where her home was. But against that, no one had ever been quite so kind to her before, certainly never since Aunt Clara's new husband in Chioggia had asked, "What are we to do with this silent, ugly brat under our feet all the time?" which was when she herself had decided for him and come away to Venice. It was clear also that the signore was in danger. There was a boy, again in Chioggia, who always had picture storybooks, and in those whenever one man followed another it always ended with trouble. Moreover, he was wealthy and generous; therefore if one did save him from something it might easily be worth a great deal of money, and money was very important. She decided that on the whole she could put up with the headache, so long as it did not get any worse.

When Signor Light Brown left the other man at Saint Mark's she had trailed him back halfway across Venice and eventually out to the Campo Santa Maria Formosa, where he had settled once more at a restaurant on the cool side of the square. By this time she was feeling very sick indeed, and the *campo* was busy and restless, but eventually she found a patch of shade from which she could catch an occasional glimpse of him between the moving people, who were all too interested in the market, the church and the old palaces to notice one small girl sitting with her knees drawn up and her head almost resting on them. She felt extremely unwell and she wished she had a hat. A hat somehow seemed to become the most important thing in the world, but they were impossibly expensive, and she felt hopelessly alone and aggrieved suddenly. She even thought of giving up, going off to find a quiet place where she could sleep. But she would never get a hat then, she told herself sternly; she would not deserve one.

It had been a long time before the signore moved. He looked angry and anxious, but at last he seemed to make up his mind about something and started off again, this time down past the church, into the maze of narrow *calli* beyond, out at San Zaccaria ferry station for the Lido and straight across to the boat. That had worried Angela too. Although she now had over a thousand lire it would not last long if she frittered it away on such frivolities as the Lido ferry. But there was no way of slipping aboard unnoticed, and in the end, sighing deeply, she had taken a ticket herself and raced aboard just as the bell rang.

Slightly cross because she felt too unwell to enjoy the trip after spending all that money, the excitement of a big ship with two decks and a sunlit panorama of the waterfront sliding past like one of her own postcards, she had been comfortably sick on the boat and only emerged from the *toletta* again as they were bumping gently at the Lido landing. Then there was a great crowd of chattering, laughing people getting off, and after a minute the signore himself pushing out through them as if he were in a hurry, and walking away purposefully to the left.

Angela had never been on the Lido before and she

had allowed herself one glance across at the glittering plate-glass and concrete hotels, the long, shady avenue with trees and banks of flowers and awnings, and then started after him. He was fifty meters ahead now, walking fast down a long, straight road which lay beside the lagoon. Before long they left the hotels behind, and then the gardens, and finally there were just trees on the right, with the water rippling up to the edge of the road on the left, and no other people at all. Only the signore, big and dark ahead, and herself—almost trotting to keep pace behind him—a small girl in this vast space of mirror-bright sea and sky and the empty road, lonely and deserted after the crowded closeness of Venice. One felt like a fly in a glass bowl.

That was where he vanished, and it happened only because she took her eyes off him for just one minute. A small airplane had risen from behind the trees with a snarling roar, and she had watched it, fascinated, turning to follow it skimming out and climbing above the lagoon. When she looked back again Signor Light Brown had gone. It was impossible, but it was true. You could see the road for a long way, and there was nothing on it at all, only in the distance the bulk of what looked like a church, flaring red against the blue sky. For a moment she had a feeling of pure panic, as if the airplane itself had swept him away by magic. But that was unlikely, and it did not even matter because after all this and spending so much money she had lost him anyhow. She went on a little way further, still hoping that somehow he might reappear; at last she dropped helplessly in the grass by the waterside and then realized after a time that she was crying.

So now she was sitting with her feet in the water thinking about her headache.

She was just deciding that she could put up with the headache if it all turned out well in the end when she heard footsteps on the road again and twisted round cautiously in the long grass to watch. Then she could have uttered a little song of thanksgiving, for it was the signore returning and heading back to town. He was different too—where he had been worried before he was smiling now—and as he passed her she thought even that she heard him chuckle. But there was no time to wonder about that; the problem now was whether to follow him again or first try to find out where he had been. And perhaps if she were quick she might even do both. She did not stop to think. Pulling on her sandals carefully because they were getting fragile, she crept through the grass to near enough where he had disappeared and slipped out onto the road.

It was really very simple then. You could see it easily from here. Beyond the trees on the right-hand side a tall iron fence and a rusted gate leaning half open. Glancing cautiously back at the signore, still in sight but retreating, Angela went over to it quickly and then stopped, peering inside. A strange dark-green place into which the long afternoon sunlight did not seem to penetrate: a thicket of overlush growth and half-obliterated paths, rows of tombs and headstones encrusted with lichen, and inscriptions and symbols on them in letters she did not understand. An ancient, forgotten graveyard. She did not like it. It seemed to be out of this world. And why had the signore come here? Why was he chuckling when he came away? One could imagine a person going to a new cemetery, where perhaps he had friends to remember—San Michele was even rather beautiful—but not to a place like this, and not to laugh. She stepped back suddenly and crossed herself, and then started to run. It might be best to follow the signore after all.

She caught up with him as he reached the hotels, where he swung suddenly to the left and turned into that magnificent avenue opposite the waterfront. There seemed to be as many people here as there were in Venice itself, and she had to work up closer to keep him in sight; but almost at once he stopped at a café-bar and dropped into a seat under the awning. That was good too, because she was very tired herself, very thirsty and the headache was worse. Only, she could not stay here. That waiter was another one who would chase her away, and she suspected that the signore had started to notice her.

Loitering elaborately across the next street, she was lucky again, for there was a much smaller place on the corner, no one sitting there, and a man of much kinder appearance standing in the doorway. But he was looking at her curiously too, and she was about to turn away nervously again when he said sharply, "Well now, sit down if you're going to." Without the faintest realization that she was making the most important decision of her life she asked, "Do you have a bottle of mineral water? A very small bottle because I have very little money."

He scowled down at her ferociously. "So that's how it is? You've frittered it all away? Ice cream and chocolate, eh?" She nodded slowly, and he went on, "So now you're feeling green. My word, you look green too. So we must see what can be done."

She settled on the edge of a chair rather gingerly, but it was an inexpressible relief to take yourself off your feet, and she could see Signor Light Brown very well from here. He was just sitting and nodding and smiling to himself. Why would any man do that after going to an old, dark graveyard? It was an impossible problem, and her own man came back then carrying a bottle and glass, setting them down on the table with a clatter and announcing, "Two Milanese. They only took half a glassful each with their *cappuccini*. They have thousand-lire notes to burn, those people." She nodded, carefully working at her own money tied up in the scrap of cotton which she used for a handkerchief, and he gave the bottle a shake to make the water sparkle again, emptied it into the glass and said, "Have it on the Milanese. You may leave a little something on the table if you wish." He was looking at her thoughtfully again and he asked, "Where is your hat? You should have a hat in this heat."

Angela felt herself flushing. "I seem to have lost it. In fact I am thinking of buying another. If I can find one to suit."

"You ladies with your hats," he grumbled. "You're too fussy with them." He turned away to serve three other children who looked, she thought enviously, as if they had quite a lot of money to spend. But the signore was still there, although he had nearly finished his drink now, and she fingered through her own money carefully and chose two five-lire pieces in case she had to leave quickly. Whatever happened now he was not going to escape her again.

He was paying the waiter; in one more minute he would be lost in the crowd, and Angela placed the two small coins by her glass and started across the street. But at that moment her own man behind suddenly called, "Hey!" and, still trying to watch the signore, she turned back with her heart sinking suddenly. One should have known that ten lire was almost nothing. She whispered, "Is it not enough?"

He was standing with one hand behind him looking down at her with a very strange expression on his face. "Oh, that?" he asked. "That is most generous, signorina. I shall keep that for good luck. But you forgot your hat." He drew out his hand, holding such a hat as Angela had never dreamed of. It was made of straw, caught up at the crown and sweeping out to a wide, soft brim, and colored in violet and green and yellow. It was the most ecstatically beautiful hat in the world.

For a moment she thought it must be a joke. She could not speak, and he said, "A German fräulein. She left it here a week since, so she won't want it now. My word, they'll all see you a mile away in that hat."

She still could not speak; it was an agonizing situation. Signor Light Brown was just moving away, yet she must try it on and look at herself once in the mirror behind the ice-cream bar. The colored shade it cast over her face was almost as beautiful as the hat itself, and she breathed, "Oh, signore . . ." There was nothing else one could say, but it was quite clear that after this nothing could ever possibly go badly again.

Chapter Three

Afternoon tea on Isola San Giorgio Piccolo was a ceremony which d'Espinal would never willingly forgo. The low pink house with its French windows, the vine pergola and the group of cypresses which sheltered dear Emilia's tower, the garden floating between the blue of the sky and the sea—all were far removed from the bustle and brilliance of Venice, although only a few miles across the lagoon. It had a slightly dated elegance which especially appealed to him; it was still somehow afternoon tea on a lawn in Hampshire when the world was still civilized. Bone china and silver, Mrs. Teestock a gracious country-house lady, Emilia Pentecost cool, poised and sophisticated—a little beyond her first youth now, but still a beautiful woman.

That technically they were all confidence tricksters did not trouble him in the least. So much depended on one's point of view. For his part he saw no harm in selling a picture which, although it might have a dubious title to age or to the name it passed under, was still a masterpiece of its sort. He had never sold a bad picture in his life, and if people chose to place an insanely inflated value merely on a signature, was that his fault? Moreover, they were a nearly ideal partnership. Judith Teestock, with her amiable interest in charitable works, an assured place in Venetian society, lending them a massive aura of respectability—sometimes lending also her not inconsiderable shrewdness to their schemes. Dear Emilia, with her strange gift of snatching, as it were, some subtlety of color or feeling back out of the ages. Himself, not without a certain grand manner and wide knowledge, quietly piling up a modest little competency in a numbered account in Switzerland.

He would be the first to admit there were problems in it. One false move would send them all crashing into the devil of a mess. And there was dear Emilia. Two years ago a bored, frustrated and even dangerous woman, seeing herself chained to this little island forever and humiliatingly dependent on Aunt Judith Teestock. Now successful and assured, set free by her own talents and more still by d'Espinal's abilities in guiding and selling them. But sooner or later—indeed sooner rather than later unless he misread the signs already—Emilia would want a closer relationship than a mere business association, and he was not by any means certain that would suit him at all. He had the profoundest admiration and affection for her, but he was, and he admitted it, an adventurer. He enjoyed the adventure for its own sake, and little as one might wish to hurt her, the time would come when he must move on again. Nevertheless for the present it was a golden afternoon.

In the shade of the vines they had the contents of Raven's file spread out between them, and Emilia was studying the photographs, Mrs. Teestock the documents. D'Espinal said, "Whether our colonel is an extremely clever man affecting to be innocent, or a very innocent one with delusions of cleverness, is a nice question. Whether he himself really believes that thing is a Michelangelo might well be another."

"Could it be?" Emilia asked.

"My dear," he protested mildly, "is it possible? It's certainly a very remarkable work. But beyond that, one cannot say. Paolo doesn't think it's merely a modern forgery." He smiled at her gently. "I propose to find out."

"But what about those attestations? Surely Niccolò Sabbioni wouldn't have been taken in? Isn't he one of the world's greatest experts?"

"He is also one of the world's greatest rascals. I assure you that had Colonel Raven really found the Sleeping Cupid at Garzeno that would have been one miracle, and the fact of Sabbioni actually telling him so another. Therefore . . ." D'Espinal stopped, brooding darkly.

"What makes it so sensational?" Mrs. Teestock asked. "Apart from Michelangelo?"

"Its history," d'Espinal told her absently. "That Michelangelo himself originally sold it as a forgery. Its passing through so many hands until it disappeared in the early seventeenth century." He went on, "It seems to have been made in 1496, on Michelangelo's return to Florence from Bologna, where he had retreated after the Medici power was broken. Lorenzo the Magnificent had then been dead for several years, his worthless son Pietro driven out, Florence at war with France, that wicked friar Savonarola raising the mobs, and Cesare Borgia scheming for power in Rome."

"Hardly a world for cupids," Mrs. Teestock observed. D'Espinal glanced at her reproachfully. He disliked being interrupted. "As you say, dear lady. But Michelangelo was in extreme poverty at that time and had to make and sell something. He offered it to one Lorenzo Popolano, another offshoot of the Medici and again worthless. This Lorenzo did not want the Cupid, but suggested that Michelangelo should 'discover' it buried in a vineyard and put it out as a classical antique. Lorenzo himself then sent the Cupid to a certain Baldassare de Milanese, who subsequently sold it to Cardinal Riario di San Giorgio for two hundred gold florins, of which Michelangelo only received thirty. And since it was Lorenzo who paid Michelangelo out, we may safely assume that he and Baldassare shared the loot. Dear me," d'Espinal sighed piously, "what rascals there are in the world."

"What rascals indeed," Emilia Pentecost said softly.

D'Espinal closed his eyes, but went on, "How Michelangelo heard of this is uncertain, but he was understandably enraged. Precisely how Cardinal Riario discovered that his pretty little cupid, so far from sleeping peacefully for a thousand years or so, was a mere modern forgery is also unknown. But Michelangelo was called to Rome to explain himself, where he offered to work for Riario but in the event was treated very badly, and Baldassare was forced to take the Cupid back. Michelangelo tried to recover it, but it is said to have passed into the possession of Cesare Borgia and ultimately to Isabella d'Este. It remained with the d'Este family until it was supposed to have been purchased on behalf of King Charles the First of England in 1631. And it has never been seen since."

"It seems to me," Mrs. Teestock announced, "that they were all a wagonload of rogues—Michelangelo included."

"But colorful," d'Espinal murmured. "Colorful, dear lady."

"What do you propose?" she asked.

"Nothing, I hope," Emilia said quickly. "Don't ask me why, Harry. I couldn't tell you, it's just a feeling I have. But I don't like this."

Judith Teestock looked at her as if she were being slightly improper. "Nonsense, Emilia. You get a little fanciful sometimes. Young Bertolli is having trouble with his boat again; Pietro says it will certainly sink under him sooner or later, and if it does it will leave a young widow and five small children. I can't think how Bertolli finds the time, out fishing all night and sitting in the bars all day. If there really is a million dollars in this we can put some part of it to very good use. I'm quite sure Harcourt can arrange something."

He looked down his nose modestly. "I suspect a million dollars. And so far the precise method escapes me, but no doubt some small stratagem will suggest itself. First, I think, a short visit to Rome. I feel one should pay his respects to dear old Niccolò Sabbioni before he passes on. For yourself, dear lady, an amiable gossip with Mrs. Messina-Silvestro about our Colonel Raven—who he is and, above all, what he does. And Emilia . . ."

"I've told you, Harry," she interrupted sharply, "I don't like it."

"My dear." He looked reproachful once more.

"Have we not already arranged several very successful little projects together? If you were to hire a car and spend a few days touring around Lake Como . . . a beautiful district, and with a hint of autumn already in the air . . ."

She laughed suddenly, a little breathlessly. "You're impossible. What exactly do you want?"

He reached over and took up several of the photostats. "A little gushing talk about your dear friend Colonel Raven who was enchanted by this place Garzeno and its surroundings, presumably sometime in the early spring. Then we have a letter here describing the Cupid, written by a Father Benito Rossi and dated August 1720. One would like to know whether that good priest ever really existed. I think we shall find that he did, and you might even come across traces of his handwriting in the church records. And this Domenico Galli." He brooded over one of the documents for a moment. "The Cupid was discovered in some part of his stabling and Raven paid him a little over three hundred pounds for it. Again almost certainly quite true. But I suspect you might discover that Galli himself has moved on to a better world."

"What do you mean?" Emilia demanded sharply again. "You mean he's been murdered?"

"Certainly not," d'Espinal said. "I mean it is an obvious gambit. Whoever planned this little frolic would see the advantage of choosing an elderly person who either will not remember the precise details or might be expected to die before he can answer any questions. A confidence trick it may be, even a truly magnificent confidence trick. But it will all be in the best possible taste. We may be quite certain that nothing so vulgar as murder is contemplated."

"You're being melodramatic, Emilia," Mrs. Teestock announced briskly. "It all sounds most interesting to me, and I shall come with you. I can talk to Clara Messina-Silvestro any time—she will tell you all you need to know about anybody in between two cups of tea. We'll have Pietro drive us. When do you propose to start, Harcourt?"

But the telephone purred softly then, and he said, "That will be old Paolo. If you will permit me, dear ladies."

Left alone, Mrs. Teestock watched Emilia still frowning slightly over the photographs. Emilia was being a little unwise, she thought, and she said softly, "My dear, if you're thinking and feeling as I fancy you are about Harcourt it won't do to cross him too much."

Emilia looked up at her sharply. "What do you mean? Is it as obvious as that?" She reached out to get a cigarette, and asked, "Let's leave it, shall we?" She went on, "But, truly, I don't like this, Judith. I don't know why. That thing looks mischievous. Or perhaps a feeling that sooner or later—"

She stopped as d'Espinal came back, smiling down benevolently at both of them. "The affair marches," he announced. "Paolo now seems to have made certain discoveries. If you're agreeable, Emilia my dear, we might persuade our good Pietro to take us across to see him again after dinner. Then I shall go to Rome tomorrow." He added to Mrs. Teestock, "And something I had almost forgotten, another little adventure today. A sad, solemn, small girl." He told them about

Angela Caterina. "I have asked Paolo's Annunzietta
to look out for her. The old lady observes nearly everything in Venice. Of course," he finished, "the child
has nothing to do with our Cupid. We shall probably
never see her again."

Icarus Polliano was in an extremely bad temper.
Tugging irritably at his dinner jacket, he studied himself in the long dressing mirror: tall and thin almost to
emaciation, a dull olive skin and lifeless eyes like
greenish-colored flints, a hard, painful mouth. He
looked near enough like death, he thought. There was
nobody now who would believe that not so long ago
people had either crossed themselves or dived for
cover when they heard his name mentioned, when he
only had to say, "Fix that . . ." Even the boys were
turning on him. They were good boys, or they had
been good boys until just lately, and he himself had
treated them like his own family. But now they were
only waiting for him to pass on so they could cut him
up. "Good-bye, Polly, you were big once but now
you're just a name—and two million bucks." That hurt
worse than the permanent pain you had, and he said
through the open door, "You're making my guts ache
again. Since when has anybody ever taken me for a
ride and got away with it?"

In the yellow-satin and gilt sitting room one was
standing at the window, the other sitting on a fragile
little settee leafing through a large glossy book which
Polliano had been studying earnestly: a history of the
Medici. Alberto Mazzoni at the window, a faint habitual smile on his lips, big and quiet like a sleepy
cat; Riccardo Castello, small and dark, now studying

those pictures with a sort of sour contempt. Ricci was cunning and his reactions sometimes unpredictable. Alberto had trouble with his brain, which made him slow in speech and thought, but he was the simple one. You could use Alberto for simple things. But they were both needling him today. Standing in the bedroom doorway, Polliano asked again, "So when has anyone ever taken me for a sucker?"

Alberto did not answer, and without looking up Ricci said, "Right now, and ever since we got to this dump." He flung the book onto the table with a crash. "For God's sake, Polly, what's got into you? You want that damned Cupid so bad, why don't we locate this guy and sweat it out of him? Or else give up and go back to Rome."

"Ricci," Polliano reminded him, "we go back to Rome when I say. It's always been like that. Remember?"

"Maybe you don't feel so good," Alberto suggested.

"That's right," Polliano agreed. "You're slow, Alberto, but you understand. I feel like hell, and it don't make my temper so nice. You should remember that too, Ricci."

"What good does this thing do you anyway?" Ricci asked. "Does it make your guts feel any better?"

Polliano turned slowly to look at him and Ricci stopped. At that moment too the telephone buzzed, and he reached out for the receiver, barking into it, "Yes? Mr. Polliano's suite. Yes, he's here," holding it out then and saying, "You." He added quickly, "Don't get steamed up, Polly. It's just we don't like this place, and we're concerned for you."

Polliano grunted, taking the telephone. But then his face became surprised suddenly. He muttered, "Well, what d'you know?" and said, "Why, yes, sure I'm still interested. Where are you now? The reception? Well, that's fine, sure we'll talk. Have the bellhop bring you up." He replaced the receiver slowly while the other two watched him; they were always watching him these days, like watching one of those old kings he was reading a lot about lately, waiting for him to go. He said, "That's the guy. He's making contact. I always said he must in the end."

To Cavalli this was the only thing he could do now. He still did not like it, but it was quite clear that unless he moved fast he might easily lose his own share of the Cupid; moreover, he had already made his own plans. There were certain quite simple pre-cautions you could take, and in any case one would have to meet these people eventually. In fact, when he came in he was agreeably surprised. The thin gray person in a dinner jacket, clearly a sick man, looked nothing like a killer or an extortionist; one had met many learned scholars who seemed less distinguished. Neither did the other two—wearing lounge suits rather better than his own—appear to be very different from any number of Roman or Milanese businessmen. It was true there was just something about them, some manner, but when Polliano himself said, "Come right in, it's real nice to meet you at last. I must tell you I was starting to get the least bit impatient," he even wondered briefly whether his own rather extreme pre-cautions had not really been a little unnecessary.

"Cavalli," he announced. "Bruno Cavalli."

"So that's fine. We're glad to know you. A drink, Mr. Cavalli? A bourbon? See to it for Mr. Cavalli, will you, Ricci? And now"—Polliano laughed painfully—"there's one thing I want you should tell me. Do you always do business this way? Just calling folks, and no names and no meetings?"

Cavalli put on a small deprecating smile. "In a delicate negotiation it is quite normal. There is an object of great value involved."

"And big money," Polliano murmured. "A million. I guess we got to talk about that, Mr. Cavalli. I been thinking." He sat down carefully and turned his dull green eyes on Cavalli. He wanted that stone baby and he meant to have it, but not at a million—nor anything like that. And this guy was simple. Besides, he had something on his mind. If he had come out into the open like this it meant he was now in a hurry to sell. One time or another he, Icarus Polliano, had fixed enough deals in very different kinds of merchandise to recognize a buyer's market when he saw one. He asked, "See here, Mr. Cavalli, how big is this baby?"

"A child of six years old. A small child." Cavalli showed the length with his hands apart. "One could, for example, lift it in one's arms," he added unwisely and, momentarily startled again by a sudden look of interest on Ricci's face, said hastily, "A strong man could."

Polliano frowned. "It seems kind of small. It don't seem much for a million bucks. See, Mr. Cavalli, now we're really talking, why don't we start again. I'll make it two fifty grand."

Cavalli had expected that too. This man was really

very naïve. Only let him feel that something was forcing them to sell quickly and he would snap like a hungry shark. At the price which one had always known he was prepared to meet. You could never defeat experience in these matters. He said reproachfully, "Signore, size is no consideration. The Cupid is a unique work of art. My principal would merely smile at two hundred and fifty thousand."

"You know what?" Polliano asked. "I get to feeling there's something phoney here. Seems you're in a sudden hurry to sell."

Cavalli smiled again. "I'll be open with you, Mr. Polliano. We are. We have another gentleman interested who also talks of a million but he wants time for the settlement, and then the Cupid must go to America. As you will know, there are certain Italian export laws which make that so much more difficult. It is a tragedy for my principal, but he must now have a quick deal. There are pressing calls on him." He lowered his voice. "A woman, I suspect—possibly a very considerable scandal." Considering the bleak Raven, that amused him too. "As among friends I feel sure that if you were to propose seven fifty we could arrange something."

The eyes were more lusterless than ever. "What if I said five hundred? And fifty grand to you if you fix it?"

"It's very little." Cavalli looked doubtful. "But perhaps I could persuade him."

Polliano smiled himself, curiously sweetly, almost womanish. "You do that. There's only one thing, though. We never seen this baby yet."

"That may be anytime you say. I suggest at the Bank of America and Italy. We produce the Cupid there; you examine it with any other expert you may care to bring." He shrugged slightly. "That is not necessary, of course, but you may wish it. If we are then agreed, you present your draft and the Cupid remains in custody of the bank until that is cleared. And finally we hand you the documents of authenticity. A very simple matter after all."

"You ain't very trusting," Polliano complained, but he reached over to pat Cavalli gently on the shoulder. "You could be right at that. Like you say, it's an object of great value. Ricci, see to our friend's glass again. Well now," he finished, "I'm sorta tied up this next two, three days. You get a lot of social engagements in a place like this. I'll be in touch. Where can we reach you, Mr. Cavalli?"

Cavalli had expected that—it was really very obvious, even rather amusing—and he said, "I have a small rented apartment, very modest, and I am often out. Perhaps I should call you? In three days?" But it would be as well to leave now, he thought; one should always know when to finish, and there was just a hint of something creeping in here.

"So soon?" Polliano asked. "Not another drink before you leave? No? Well, it's been a real pleasure. I'll have Alberto see you down." He waved away Cavalli's protest. "It's a big place. You might get lost."

Stopping at the door, Cavalli looked back. The sweet, sensitive smile again seemed quite friendly, and he felt that perhaps he had merely imagined that touch of menace a moment past. There was still one thing he wanted to know. Why did Polliano want the Cupid? Cavalli had noticed that big book on the Medici and it could even be that Polliano was thinking of starting a collection, in which case there were so many other things to sell him. But seeing Ricci watching him, Cavalli suddenly thought better of asking. He glanced at Alberto, holding the door open for him, and finished, "Then we shall be in touch, Mr. Polliano?"

"Sure," Polliano agreed softly. "Sure, Mr. Cavalli. We'll be in touch."

Ricci watched it close after them and whispered incredulously, "Jeez. That's the guy takes us for suckers. Listen, Polly, you want that stone baby, so let me and Alberto get it for you. But for God's sake, half a million bucks—"

"Ricci," Polliano told him, "you don't have no psychology, you should read a book sometime. It's good to keep folks happy, and Mr. Cavalli wants to talk about half a million, so why not?" He crossed over to the cocktail cabinet and carefully poured a small tot of brandy. "My stomach's a whole lot better all of a sudden. Mr. Cavalli's a kinda nice guy, though maybe a bit simple. I know just how much I'll give him for the baby when we get around to it. But just for now you go down, catch Alberto in the reception and then the both of you tail the little man. He's sorta coy about where he lives. I get a feeling he don't trust us, and that ain't nice, Ricci."

Across the wide roadway of the Lungomare Marconi, her bright hat flaring in the early evening sunshine, Angela Caterina sat on a bench by the autobus stop looking even more solemn than usual. Her headache was better now, but she was getting hungry again. She was enjoying the spectacle of the never-ending stream of elegant automobiles and the shabby though somehow frivolous horse carriages with their sunshades, but still patiently watching the white marble steps and the chrome-and-glass doors of the big luxury hotel opposite, and thinking that it was a long walk back to the ferryboat station.

Chapter Four

When the ferry stopped back in Venice once more, Angela waited for the signore to go ashore first. She was getting careful. She was almost certain that he had looked across at her curiously from the hotel steps and again on the boat, but she was quite certain he did not realize that two other men were also following him now. She herself had seen them several times: coming out of the hotel itself, edging through the crowd in the Gran Viale, finally taking a water taxi at the Elisabetta steps just as the ferry was moving out and roaring away into the darkening lagoon on wide white wings of spray. So they would reach Venice long before the ferry and could be waiting for the signore when he landed. But he had seemed quite unconscious of them, sitting in the forward saloon with a glass of wine and still looking very pleased with himself.

It was getting dark now and the lamps were coming on; the arches of the palace illuminated with soft yellow light, the white bridges, the colored dresses of the ladies on the pavement and the boats all seeming to float on a glittering, flashing sea of reflections, like fireworks. But there was no time for such fancies. Signor Light Brown was already crossing the riva and, sure enough, the other two men appeared silently from somewhere behind a news vendor's kiosk and fell in after him. She felt a sudden little touch of fear. If the signore was going into those dark, narrow *calli* beyond the waterfront, almost anything might happen.

Nevertheless this was too exciting to miss. She slipped along after them like a small shadow, and in a few minutes they left people and lights behind as if going into another and darker world, through one silent passage after another, with the signore moving on steadily and the other two following him from corner to corner, keeping him in sight but never trying to catch up. At last he turned into an even narrower *calle*—little more than a tunnel, with an archway at the far end—remained silhouetted against the dim yellow light beyond for a second and then vanished.

Angela knew exactly where they were; she often came here herself. It was a dark little enclosed courtyard: the Campo Sant' Anna. On this side a high blank wall with just the one archway, opposite an old building which had been made over into apartments. To the right a deserted canal, again with tall buildings on the far side, and on the left the back of an ancient, empty palace, closed and boarded up—one of her own special places which she had often explored from top to bottom. She even sometimes slept up there in an angle of the roof during the afternoons, though never at night because she suspected there might be ghosts here.

But she could get no further because the two men themselves had stopped in the archway, apparently watching from there. So unless she could get a little closer herself, to peep through that opening, she might lose the signore again. Moreover, they were talking too, their voices whispering along the walls, and it was clearly terribly important to hear what they were saying; it might explain everything. More excited than afraid, she crept closer, close enough to hear the smaller one mutter, "So that's it. First floor, the balcony."

"Listen, Ricci," the other asked, "why don't we go in right now? Maybe the baby's there."

"Polly don't want it that way," Ricci said.

The big man grunted. "Polly's nuts—and sick. Maybe sometime soon it has to be the way we want it. Polly wants that baby, so we get it for him. That guy says a strong man can carry it. So I'm a strong man. Then we tell Polly you got your goddamn baby, so now we beat it out of this dump."

"Take it easy," Ricci started, but then checked and looked over his shoulder. He swung round suddenly. Angela was close enough to see the glint of his eyes in the lamplight. She turned wildly to run, took only one step, felt her ruinous old sandals catching at a loose flagstone and fell helplessly. Half dazed, she was just conscious of the big one moving as swiftly as a cat, one hand dragging her up and another clamping over her mouth as she opened it to scream. It seemed to be a year, hanging there in the half-darkness, and then Ricci clutched at her shoulder, shaking her savagely and whispering through his teeth, "What're you doing here?"

The other said, "It's only a kid." He dragged her out into the courtyard, under the light, and peered down at her. "A kinda no-account kid."

"No-account, hell." Ricci shook her again, and she

clutched desperately at her precious hat. "I seen her before. I seen that hat. Away back on the Lido, and coming off the ferry. The little bastard's tailing us."

Angela began to cry. "I am not, I am not. It is the other signore. I do not even know his name . . ." She lied hopelessly. "I was going to rob him. Take something from his pockets. I am very poor and I often do it."

The big one bent down until his face was almost touching hers. "You're kinda small for that." His voice was soft but it frightened her still more. "See here, kid, you come clean and maybe we give you something. Or if you don't, maybe we beat the hell out of you."

"Signore," Angela wept. She prayed: "Please Holy Mother and Sant' Anna . . . I am not following you, I am only looking for someplace to sleep, and I do not care about the baby."

She caught her breath, realizing her mistake too late, and Ricci whispered, "What? What d'you know about the baby? You tell me now or by . . ."

He twisted her head back, but the other one interrupted urgently, "Hold it, Ricci! Folks!"

They both froze suddenly, listening to the footsteps at the other end of the tunnel. There were two people: a woman speaking angrily and a man laughing, saying, "Don't get worried," and calling out, "Hey there, where are we? Do you know? How do we find the Grand Canal?" Ricci cursed under his breath but the fingers relaxed slightly, just enough for Angela to twist away, feeling him snatch after her and the collar of her shirt tearing, then clutching her hat and running blindly for the old palace whether there were ghosts in it or not.

Another second and she was wrenching the loose board back from a ground-floor window. One more and she was crouching in the hot, musty darkness inside and peering out at the courtyard, watching the man and woman move across towards the canal, with Ricci and the other still standing by the archway and looking across at the palace. They seemed to be arguing, but at last the big one turned away, back into the tunnel, and Ricci followed him. Then she wiped her nose fiercely with the back of her hand and told herself for the second time today that crying was very foolish. She was really doing very well; there was no doubt that she had been allowed a Heaven-sent escape, which in itself proved she was doing the right thing. Equally there was no doubt that this was a very dark business, and now all of a sudden there was a surprising baby in it. Perhaps Heaven was using her to look after that baby too. So the problem was: what ought she to do next? Also, she was extremely hungry again.

While she was thinking about it the big clock of the Orologio away over Saint Mark's Square boomed out nine slow strokes, which were answered by one church after another. The courtyard was very quiet, but in here the old palace had its own sounds: a soft creak like someone walking in the rooms above, the rustle perhaps of something drifting down, from somewhere the lap and ripple of water, and then a movement in the darkness only a few feet away. She was not exactly frightened but, still, she did not like it. And she had made up her mind anyway. It was really very simple. One signore had given her money and a lot to eat only for telling him that he was being followed, and so might this other. She was quite sure now that he could not really be a bad man, not if those others were against him. Besides, she wanted to know about that baby.

Out in the courtyard there was no sign of anything moving. In the apartment building two windows were glowing high up under the eaves and another on the first floor. That was what Ricci had said: "First floor, the balcony." Angela could see it all quite clearly from here: an opening from the pavement and a flight of steps inside, a stone balcony and there at the end a modern door with a square pane of glass. With one more look across at the canal and at the archway in the wall she edged out cautiously, but nothing moved.

At first there was no answer to the doorbell. But then a shadow fell across the glass and the signore asked, "Who is it?" He sounded nervous and she answered, "If you please, it is very important." The door opened a few inches then, with Signor Light Brown there, staring down at her. She was half tempted to run away herself, but she repeated, "If you please . . ." and he whispered, "So, you again? I have seen you before today, several times—you have been following me, in fact." Before Angela could step back he too reached out and took her shoulder. He said, "Come in, little girl."

On the balcony in Paolo's garden the table was a pool of light under an angle lamp, the photographs again spread out on it, Paolo's books opened and flattened at illustrations, the old man himself with his heavy magnifying glass, d'Espinal and Emilia Pentecost leaning over. They were all very quiet. Somewhere in the background Annunzietta was grumbling, "That's all very well, such an opera. Will you clear that away and let me bring you fresh coffee?" A big dark moth was circling in the brilliance and the cat Isabella d'Este was sitting on the arm of a chair with her head slightly to one side and studying these strange proceedings suspiciously.

Paolo was saying, "You see this detail in the Cupid? The treatment of the hair—quite typical. Here it is again," giving d'Espinal the glass and pulling over one of the books. "The Tomb of the Savelli, reputedly by Mino da Fiesole, which is, or was, in the Boston Museum of Fine Arts. Here again in the Madonna and Child, at one time thought to be by Pisano, and at one time acquired by the Cleveland Museum. Once more again an echo of it in the Athene."

D'Espinal studied each of the illustrations in turn before straightening up. "You make your point, old friend. So what it comes to is the same handwriting in half a dozen other masterpieces."

"I think so," Paolo said. "The modeling of the eyes. Here . . . and here. The lips also. You see in this other child nearly the same growing smile, the hint of mischief."

"You feel that too?" Emilia asked quickly.

There was a faint touch of impatience in d'Espinal's voice. "The mischief is in the artist, my dear, not in the work he creates." He looked at Paolo. "So our conclusion?"

Paolo shook his head and posed one of his habitual conundrum questions. "What is a conclusion? The possibility, rather. That your Cupid there was carved sometime between 1918 and 1928. It was carved in Rome. And it was carved by a man named Alceo Dossena."

He smiled up at Emilia, pleased with his detective work, and she asked, "But who was Alceo Dossena?"

The old man closed one of his books gently and pushed it away. "At that time a superb artist—in the tradition of hundreds of generations of Italian artist-craftsmen—who worked in a little studio by the Tiber, not far from the Castel Sant' Angelo in Rome. As to what he was, that is another matter."

"A supreme forger or an incredibly naïve genius," d'Espinal murmured. "He created works of all periods, from Greek to Gothic and High Renaissance, all accepted as perfectly genuine by experts and museums everywhere. And he claimed afterwards that he did not realize they were being sold as such. It's a long story." He chuckled faintly. "He also created one of the biggest scandals ever to shake the world of art. I begin to see as through a glass, darkly. How old is Sabbioni, Paolo? Eighty-two? Then he would have been in his thirties when Dossena was working. And his father was Giulio Sabbioni, the dealer in antique sculpture."

"I see the inference. It's no more than that."

"He could have known Dossena," d'Espinal insisted heavily. "He almost certainly did."

"It still doesn't explain away the scientific tests," Emilia argued. "They're by separate, disinterested people. They can't be falsified."

D'Espinal sounded slightly impatient again. "Dear lady, that's really quite simple. Dossena would have carved the Cupid out of a very much larger work of the same period. Something relatively worthless. There was plenty to be found at one time, and it's been done before." He went on, "Dear me, what a fascinating conversation I shall have with that ancient rascal, Niccolò. If only one half of what I suspect about this affair is true he must be growing worse as he grows older."

Emilia got up abruptly. "We should be leaving," she said. "I'll try to entice Pietro away from old Andreas."

Paolo watched her going down the balcony steps, calling back good night to Annunzietta, the old lady coming out to her still offering to bring fresh coffee. "You might be wiser to take Signorina Emilia to Paris," he suggested mildly. "One imagines she would like it better too. But if you're determined, and if I think of anything more, I'll ask Annunzietta to meet you at the air terminal tomorrow."

The signore locked the door carefully. It was a small bright and shining kitchen with gleaming metal and white enamel, and a faint but beautiful scent of bread and coffee. Beyond the other open doorway Angela could see a short, tiled passage and three more doors, but there was no sound or movement from them, and she was sure that the apartment was empty except for the signore and herself. There was certainly no sign of a baby. She knew that at once because in Chioggia one had a lot of experience with these things: a baby always made its presence perfectly obvious anywhere.

So what had those men been talking about? After the long day, especially the last hour or so, she was starting to feel a little confused.

He said, "You are a beggar."

Sitting on the kitchen stool, afraid she might fall off if she were not careful, Angela shook her head slowly. "Your pardon, signore, but I am not. I sell postcards."

"You are a beggar," he repeated. "And do you know what the police do with beggars? They put them in the Old Prison over the Bridge of Sighs. So now then, why have you been following me all day? What d'you want?"

Angela looked at him warily. Perhaps she had been foolish to come up here after all—she had heard terrible stories about that place over the Bridge of Sighs. She sniffled slightly and said, "I don't often cry, but I have cried twice today already. Perhaps because I'm very tired—and hungry. I came only to tell the signore that there were two men following him. From the Lido, and then they took a taxi, and again on the Riva Schiavoni . . ."

She stopped suddenly, really frightened by the look on his face. He bent down close to her, whispering, "What? What are you saying? You are not lying? If you are, this is not a game."

"I am not lying," Angela insisted. She told him carefully and slowly, starting from her wait outside the Hotel Ludovico Manin, and he listened, nodding and staring at her, cursing softly once or twice. "They are going to kill your baby," she finished, looking round the bright, impersonal little kitchen. "But you have no baby here. One can always tell."

"No baby here," he repeated. "Dear God," he asked, "am I, Bruno Cavalli, a fool?"

"I am very hungry," she reminded him, sensing somehow that at least for this moment things were different.

"Hungry?" he asked. "Yes, of course. Little girls are always hungry." Wrenching open a big white enameled door, he went on in short bursts, "Now you sit there. Sit quite still. Don't try to run away." He was bringing out cheese and bread, sausage, milk and grapes, and she thought complacently that it was really all very easy and she had no intention of running away—at least not yet. He was cursing again, calling himself a fool and muttering something about the baby again, while he carved hunks of bread into a basket and filled a beaker of milk. He said angrily. "So eat. After that we must talk. What is your name?"

Hesitating about whether to start first on the sausage or the cheese, she said absently, "Angela Caterina."

"Where do you come from?"

But nothing was going to make her tell that she only came from Chioggia, just across the water, where it would be so easy to send her back, so she murmured, "A long way."

"And don't you have a mama and papa?"

She finished the first slice of sausage and reached for another. "My papa drove a big truck and he went off one day for Milan, and then Rome. But he did not come back, so my mama went to look for him and she did not come back either, so I went to live with my aunt. But then she married a man and he did not like me. He said I was ugly and silent, and I came away."

Cavalli whispered, "Dear God," but the sausage was beautiful and he did not seem to mind how much she ate. "So you are alone?" he asked. "No one knows where you are?"

"Quite alone," she admitted. "But I do very well. Today in particular. Today I have a hat, and if I continue to do well I shall get new sandals soon." She glanced at him sideways. "As you can see, I need them. But they are terribly expensive." She waited, but he did not answer, and she said, "I could work for the money. I could watch for those other two men. Or better still, look after your baby."

"Don't keep talking about the baby!" he shouted suddenly. "Be quiet and let me think. Eat!" He sat down himself, staring at her and muttering again. It frightened Angela. Someone really ought to tell him that talking to yourself was the worst possible of all bad luck. "Dear God," he whispered, "I should have thought of that. It was so simple. There is only one thing now, as I decided. But I cannot, I must not leave Venice. I lose everything if I do. Hell's damnation on that colonel—and Sabbioni!" This, Angela thought, was inexpressibly wicked—and foolish.

Then he spoke to her again, angrily. "Now then, why have you been following me? And don't lie. That hat. You probably stole it, but it's a very foolish hat. Anybody can see you from a mile away." He leaned closer to her across the table. "Who is paying you for this, and why?"

"It's a beautiful hat and I did not steal it and I was not following you. It only happened that way." She finished desperately: "I think I should go now."

"Go where?"

"Where I sleep. I am very tired. There is a place in the Exposition Gardens. Or I know a man who has a boat with a cover on it."

He asked, "Do you know what happens to little girls who sleep like that? Today on the Piazza San Marco you were talking to another signore, a big man who walks as if he owns Venice. His name is d'Espinal. Do you know that?" She did not answer and he slapped the table top with the palm of his hand. "What were you talking about? Did he speak of a cupid?"

Angela blinked at him. "Please, what is a cupid?"

"No," Cavalli muttered, "he wouldn't. Not to a child. I'm really being very foolish." He was sweating and he snatched at a towel to mop his face. "So did he tell you to follow me?"

"No, signore. He said I must not."

"I do not understand this," he complained. He seemed almost to forget she was there, and she started to slide down off the stool, but he barked, "Sit still! I might have something for you yet. This man you know, with a boat. Who is he?"

Angela did not understand that either but she said, "His name is Mario. He works from the markets bringing fish and vegetables to the hotels in the very early morning."

Cavalli nodded and then appeared to forget her again, whispering something to himself which this time she could not catch. At last he said, "Very well, then. Fetch him."

She looked at him doubtfully. "Now? What for?"

"What is that to do with you?" he shouted. "Bring him back here. Say I have work for him and I shall pay well."

"If I do will you give me something? A thousand lire?" she suggested tentatively.

He almost screamed at her. "A thousand what! And

after feeding you?" He caught her shoulder again and shook her. "Listen, you little fool. Do you know who those men were? Mafiosi. D'you know what that means?" She nodded doubtfully. "They'd cut your throat as soon as look at you. And mine." He stopped and then went on rather sadly, "Once they've seen you they'll never forget. They're bad enemies, those people. Now fetch this Mario. I want him here within the hour."

The glittering water-buses and ferryboats behind them, a glowing cruise ship slipping silently out to the Porto di Lido and the open sea, they were turning into the darker, quieter waters of the northern lagoon with the lamps of Venice swinging away in a long string on their left and the softer lights of Murano low down ahead in the darkness. Emilia Pentecost watched them for a time, thinking that life on San Giorgio Piccolo had become very pleasant since this great, amusing, infinitely captivating rogue had joined them there. She wondered how long it would last, how long it could last, indeed. Glancing sideways at him sitting beside her in the rear cockpit, with Pietro stolidly at the wheel, she asked, "Harry, what exactly are you planning? To steal this thing?"

"Purloin," he murmured, rather as if the other word were just a shade vulgar. "It is a diverting possibility. One suspects that nobody's title to the Cupid is particularly sound. The pretty child may be picked up by the roadside, as it were, as our good colonel is supposed to have found it."

"But how? Don't you feel that might be dangerous?"

He was slightly reproachful. "Nothing crude is contemplated."

She did not say anything for some time again, now watching the lights of Murano falling abeam. Pietro was speeding up; they would be home in a few minutes. She said suddenly, "Harry—about ourselves . . ."

He moved, and Emilia could just see him looking at her in the watery half-light. "Yes, my dear, about ourselves?" For d'Espinal he sounded uneasy. "You're thinking about your little Bassano?"

"Not exactly." She laughed in her curiously attractive, breathless way. "I was thinking I've changed a lot in this last few months, and wondering . . . It doesn't matter. I suppose you'll have to meet this person, Polliano?"

He seemed relieved by the change of subject, she thought. "With a million dollars in the air it would be recklessly careless not to. I love a simple old-fashioned millionaire."

D'Espinal might not have loved Icarus Polliano at that moment, however. He was in the Municipal Casino playing the roulette tables and losing ill-temperedly. It was another affront to him. There was a time when he would not have lost; this was just one more thing which was against him, like Ricci and Alberto. Several times in the last few days he had thought quietly to give up this damned baby and go home—it had only been a sick fancy from the start. Like Ricci said, he could not think what had got into him. But Ricci was the wrong one to say that. Nobody hustled Icarus Polliano, and what's more, nobody took him for a ride. He meant to have that Cupid now, sick or not, and he meant to have it in his own time and his own way. So when Ricci and Alberto appeared through the crowd in the gaming salon and stood silently behind him as if they were his keepers, he watched five more five-thousand lire chips being raked in without speaking and then looked over his shoulder wickedly. "You been long enough about it."

"Don't get steamed up," Ricci said. "We got the guy located. He's in some place as quiet as a morgue. Listen, Polly, we go over anytime we like and collect that baby."

Icarus placed five more chips in a careful pattern. "I keep telling you, I don't want it that way." He watched those chips being swept away too. "So you locate this Cavalli. So you're smart. Were you smart enough to let him see you?"

"Not Cavalli didn't. But some kid did. I've kinda got that kid on my mind," Alberto muttered.

"Why d'you bring that up?" Ricci asked. "You let the little bastard get away."

"Okay," Polliano said wearily, "so there's a kid in it now. I don't ask why. Seems it's getting sorta humorous. Maybe we'll have a big fat man next. God's sake," he snapped, "you know what to do with kids, don't you? There's plenty of water about. Let's get outta here. This ain't my night."

"It might pay off, at that," Alberto muttered. "I been thinking about that kid. I reckon she's trouble. I'd like to guess what she's doing next."

In fact Angela was crouching in her hiding place in the old palace and too aggrieved to worry much about the ghosts. She was watching Signor Cavalli's apartment. After a great deal of trouble she had found Mario, slightly drunk and very obstinate, in one of the

bars near the fish market; with still more she had persuaded him to come back with her all the way across
the Rialto Bridge, arguing that there would be thousands and thousands of lire in it for him. Then, when
she had at last got him here and quite politely suggested only one thousand for her own trouble, the
signore had simply laughed at her. He had produced
a bottle of wine for himself and Mario and driven her
away, saying, "Go and see what your other friend,
Signor d'Espinal, is doing." It was really too much,
and she was determined now to find out what was
happening.

In a few minutes Mario came out again, hurrying
across the campo, with Signor Cavalli watching him
from the balcony. After that, uncomfortable as she
was, Angela nearly went to sleep until she heard the
engine of a boat on the canal and blinked her eyes
open fiercely to see Mario once more disappearing into
the apartment. This time he reappeared quickly, followed by Signor Cavalli carrying something in his
arms—something draped in a white sheet—and carrying it exactly as one would carry a heavy child.

Angela felt a touch of pure horror. That would be
the baby, of course. And to be carrying it like that, so
stiffly and all wrapped up, clearly it must be dead. She
understood now why she had felt sure there was no
other living person in the apartment and why Signor
Cavalli had been so frightened. Out there in the dimly
lit campo even Mario seemed to be uneasy, but Signor
Cavalli went on steadily towards the canal. They
faded into the shadows over there, although she could
still see the glimmer of the white sheet, and then the
engine started up and the tiny prow light of the boat

moved slowly along the canal to the left. That would bring them into the Rio dei Mendicanti and out into the Laguna Morta. The Lagoon of the Dead. So were they just going to drop that baby into the water there?

The sound died away, and after that it was very quiet. A marauding cat crept out from somewhere and vanished again, a whisp of paper danced over the flagstones in a sudden little breeze and all the clocks started to chime. It was one o'clock and Angela crept out cautiously. She did not like this place any more. Her hut in the Exposition Gardens suddenly seemed to be inexpressibly desirable and secure. But she would certainly find Mario tomorrow; even if she could not get him to give her something she would certainly make him tell her all about it.

Chapter Five

Angela had slept late and been turned out of the hut by one of the gardeners coming to work; when she reached the markets all the early porterage was finished and she could not find Mario anywhere. His boat was in the usual place but nobody had seen him that morning, and one of the men said perhaps he'd won the lottery, he must be in the money to duck his work like this. Angela thought peevishly that he almost certainly was, and she had wasted a long walk all across the city; but she managed to wheedle an apple and a very small bunch of old grapes from one of the stall holders, and then went and sat on the market steps to eat them and think out what to do next.

She counted her money first. Just over nine hundred lire now, which was nine hundred more than she had this time yesterday but still not very much; it seemed that once you started getting money you had to go on getting a great deal more before it was really any use to you. The only problem was how. There was something her aunt's new husband in Chioggia often said: if you knew enough you could always find someone ready to pay for it. So she really knew quite a lot now, and of course the person most likely to pay her best was the big English signore. Morever, he would know what to do about Signor Cavalli taking his poor baby out to the Laguna Morta. She herself was not going anywhere near the police—that was much too dangerous. But she would have to find Signor d'Espinal, which might be difficult, and it was going to be very hot again. She sighed gently, and at that point someone behind her asked, "Is your name Angela Caterina?"

She turned to see a boy carrying a marketing basket and an incredibly ancient lady looking down at her. The old lady said, "A fine scarecrow you are," went on to the boy, " 'Como, call that gondola. Then you may take the basket back to the gallery," and while he put his fingers into his mouth to emit a piercing whistle, she added to Angela, "You must come with me. Get in now, child, quickly," and told the gondolier, "The air terminal."

Half poised for flight, torn between not liking the look of this old lady, curiosity and the thrill of riding in a gondola, Angela whispered, "Why? Not to an airplane?"

The old lady settled herself carefully, looking at Angela out of sharp black eyes. "We are going to meet Signor d'Espinal. He told me to look out for you."

"Then that will do very well," Angela said. "I want to meet the signore, too."

"I've no doubt," Annunzietta commented dryly. "He's a very generous gentleman." She went on studying Angela disapprovingly and asked, "Did you steal that hat?"

"I did not," Angela protested. "People must not keep on saying that. It was given to me by another very kind man."

"It's easy to see the way you're going," Annunzietta said. "It's too gaudy. And your clothes need washing.

You're half starved, child, and obstinate with it too, by the look of you."

"Please," Angela told her, "I eat when I can."

It really was a very sharp old woman, Angela thought; there were lots like her in Chioggia, the old grandmothers, and they imagined they could rule everybody. But it was worth putting up with to get to the signore so easily. This gondola was saving a lot of wear on her sandals, and the spectacle of the Grand Canal, the colored palaces floating by and the gleaming boats and launches skimming past them was really quite enchanting. She settled down to watch it silently.

When they got to the crowd which was always fussing about the air terminal steps the signore was already there. He helped the old lady from the gondola, saying, "As beautiful as ever, Annunzietta."

She cackled with laughter at that as if it were an old joke and told him, "You never grow any better. Before I forget, the padrone says you are to ask Niccolò Sabbioni whether he ever knew a person named Alfredo Fasoli—a goldsmith. Also, there is a book for you to read on the airplane." She produced that from her bag, and finished, "And I myself have found you this," nodding at Angela.

D'Espinal smiled down at her. "I see you have. What a superb hat, Angela Caterina. How are you?"

"I still do very well," she said. "I have a great deal to tell you."

"And it will no doubt be important. But I have very little time now." He looked at the old lady. "What are we to do with her, 'Etta? Signora Teestock and

Signorina Emilia are themselves away for a few days."

"She must come back with me," Annunzietta said. "The padrone takes in half the stray cats of Venice, and one stray child will be little more. I shall give her a bath," she announced with some relish. "A good scrubbing. And wash those filthy clothes."

"Signore," Angela insisted, "I have to tell you the most serious things."

"Even they must wait. You see that beautiful but stern lady?" He nodded towards a brisk young woman in airline uniform already marshaling her flock to a motor launch. "She is obviously a princess in disguise who is going to take me to Rome, and she will be most annoyed if I keep her waiting."

Angela tried again desperately. "It is about the light-brown signore and two other very bad men and the baby."

"The baby?" d'Espinal repeated. He looked puzzled and started to ask, "What—" but the stewardess behind them said, "If you are taking this flight to Rome, signore," and he promised, "Tomorrow, Angela. I shall be back in the afternoon and you can tell me then." He produced a five-hundred-lire piece, saying, "In the meantime you may need this for urgent expenses."

He vanished into the motor launch before Angela could think of anything else to say, and but for the good solid coin clutched in her hand she could have wept with frustration. She watched the big boat moving out into the canal before she turned away disconsolately, and then the old lady commanded, "Come along then, child."

That was impossible too. Looking, as Annunzietta told Paolo afterwards, more mulish than ever, Angela said, "You are very kind, signorina, and thank you for the ride in the gondola, but if you will forgive me I think I shall stay here." She slipped away into the crowd. Annunzietta had no hope of stopping her and, almost before the old lady quite realized she had gone, Angela disappeared among the silks and souvenir stalls, thinking obstinately: I will not have them send me back to Chioggia, and I will not have all this talk about washing and scrubbing.

At least she was five hundred lire better off, but she still had the problem of what to do next. Not look again for Mario, she thought, because if he had made a lot of money last night he would probably be magnificently drunk by now. That left only Signor Cavalli —but was it quite safe? If he took a dead baby out into the Laguna Morta at one o'clock in the morning he might not think twice about her either. Yet somehow she could not quite believe that now. He was not as generous or so comfortable as Harcourt d'Espinal, but she could not really think he was that sort of man, although the others might be. It was at this point that she started to wonder vaguely whether that baby was a real child after all. Also, Signor Cavalli had told her last night to go and find out what her other friend was doing. So she had, and it might even be worth a few more lire for telling him. She set out doggedly for the Campo Sant' Anna.

When she got to the courtyard it was still silent and deserted. Only a gaunt yellow cat, stealing out of her own hiding place in the old palace, watched her suspiciously as she went across and up the steps. Again the signore was a long time coming to the door, but at last it jerked open a few inches. He looked bad-tempered, his clothes were more crumpled than ever and he grunted, "You again?"

"If you please," Angela reminded him, "you said to find out what the English signore is doing. Well, I have."

There was a beautiful smell of coffee wafting through the open doorway, and he stared at her for a moment and then asked, "You have, eh? Well then, come in. You amuse me, though God knows why. You are a singularly ugly child." Angela knew that quite well herself, so there was nothing to say about it, and he did not look amused. He said, "I suppose you're still hungry? So sit down, then. Don't you ever smile?" She did not answer that either, and he poured her a big bowl of coffee, saying, "Here," and then, "So what is d'Espinal doing?"

"I would like some bread too," Angela told him. "And I have walked a long way today already. My sandals are almost falling off my feet."

Cavalli stopped in the act of buttering a piece of bread himself and laughed, rather jarringly. "What d'you want? Money?" She nodded and he laughed again and took out a note, holding it up between his finger and thumb.

It was a thousand lire, and she said, "He has gone to Rome to see a person named Niccolò Sabbioni and he is to ask this person whether he ever knew another one named Alfredo Fasoli, a goldsmith."

The effect startled and frightened Angela. Cavalli stared at her again, rather horribly this time. The note slipped from his fingers and lay on the table between them. "What did you say?" he whispered. "Where did you get that from? Tell me now—all of it." With her eyes on the note Angela explained carefully. It did not sound like so very much after all, but when she finished Cavalli said angrily, "Well then, take it. It's all you think about, money and eating. Now listen and consider. Was there another name? Dossena? Alceo Dossena?"

She was already folding the note lovingly, pushing it into her pocket, and she shook her head. "I did not hear that one."

"You're sure," he insisted, and then fell back into his dangerous habit of talking to himself, whispering, "It can only mean that d'Espinal knows—or suspects. But in God's name how did he find out? And does Raven himself . . . ?"

He stopped, as if looking at something which Angela could not see. She reached out for another piece of bread, dipping it into her coffee, and asked carefully, "Is it about the baby, signore? Signore, why is it such a heavy baby?"

"Because it's made of stone, you little fool," he answered automatically, and then shouted, "What's it got to do with you? What're you prying for, eh? You'll get yourself into trouble, girl. You'll get your throat cut if you're not careful, and nobody will miss you. You forget that baby." He went on more calmly, "It's very dangerous. Now then, what else did d'Espinal say?"

"Nothing," she protested, "truly nothing at all. Except he is coming back from Rome tomorrow."

"Tomorrow," Cavalli repeated. Still watching Angela, he nodded suddenly. "Now pay attention. Signor Harcourt d'Espinal lives on Isola San Giorgio Piccolo, and there is a woman there who is interested in helping the poor. Very well, then. You are poor, so she will help you. I want you to go to San Giorgio."

Angela finished her coffee first and then said, "No. I know people like that. They'll want to send me back where I come from."

"I could easily send you back myself," Cavalli threatened. "If you annoy me I could have every policeman in Venice looking for you. Come now, you need only meet Signor d'Espinal at the air terminal tomorrow. Tell him some sad story, but go back with him to San Giorgio. It should be quite easy. And while you are there I want you to watch everything and listen to everything. Also, I think there is a studio there, a place where people paint pictures. So I want you to look at the pictures in that studio and remember them. Whether they look old or new and what they are about. Can you do that?"

"Quite easily," she said. "But I don't want to. How do I get away again?"

"You're a clever girl. You can think of something. They can't keep you there if you don't want to stay. So you come back to me and tell me all about it, and I shall give you a lot of money."

"How much?" she asked. "Enough for new sandals?"

"More than enough. It could be as much as five thousand." He screwed up his eyes thoughtfully. "You should get to the island tomorrow and come back the day after. So I want you here the day after tomorrow at eight o'clock in the evening."

He seemed to be pleased suddenly. He said, "You are a serious little girl. I like that," and found a paper bag from somewhere, packing the bread into it, cheese, almost half a chicken, adding apples and a bunch of grapes, while Angela watched him with her eyes as round as saucers. "You must go now," he told her finally. "I have business myself. But you see I can treat people well when they work with me. There is only one more thing," he added, holding her arm suddenly. "You must never, never speak of the baby again. Someone might easily kill you if you do. Do you understand?"

"I wouldn't be at all surprised," Angela admitted. "Not with those other men."

"That is what I mean. Now then, off you go. And remember—the day after tomorrow at eight o'clock."

It was very quiet in Colonel Raven's study. The same greenish light from the windows and the same damned water ripples dancing monotonously on the ceiling, the colonel himself still sitting in his high-backed chair. But he was very angry today and, Cavalli thought with some amusement, quite helpless. Raven slapped his hand down with a sharp crack on the desk. He snapped, "Don't play the fool, Cavalli. Where is it?"

Cavalli shook his head. "Hidden. And if anything should happen to me it will probably never be found again." His eyes were uneasy, but he was enjoying this in his own way.

"For God's sake, man, why all this tortuous scheming?"

"I thought if there came an event when someone—perhaps two or three very ugly men, or even yourself—decided to come to my apartment, I did not want the Cupid found there. One must always have a little personal insurance. Also, I do not choose to be driven out by this Harcourt d'Espinal. And so long as only I know where the Cupid is, I can't be."

"Let's talk like reasonable people," Raven suggested. "You say Polliano is dangerous. I don't agree, but you may be right. Very well, then. If anyone has to get in trouble, why not let it be d'Espinal himself?"

"I have not the smallest objection in the world. But in that case there would be nothing in it for me. And nothing for you either. With respect, Colonel, you do not appear to think about these things very clearly."

Raven took a deep, hard breath, but got up and crossed to the side table, where there was a silver tray with decanters and glasses. He asked, "Scotch?"

"I rarely take anything more than a little Campari seltzer," Cavalli said. He went on, "In a minute I will tell you something about this d'Espinal. But first, what I have already done. I have seen Polliano himself, and we have agreed on half a million dollars."

"I'll be damned if we have," Raven snapped. "The thing's worth far more, and you know it."

"Any work of art is worth only what it will fetch." Cavalli seemed to take on an air of authority when talking about his own business. "I have already said, if one has experience there is a point at which one knows the client is prepared to deal. We have reached that point with Polliano." He sounded doubtful again, even slightly petulant. "But he wants a few more days and I do not quite like that. And I wish we knew what he wants the Cupid for."

"Does it matter?" Raven asked.

"To the extent that we could judge his sincerity.

However, I have made certain arrangements with the Bank of America and Italy against the time he does come to a conclusion—if he does. They should be safe enough, and quite effective."

"Unless I disagree," Raven commented sourly.

"In that case you have one alternative." Cavalli appeared to be studying his fingertips. "That you shall pay me one hundred thousand dollars. When I will return the Cupid to you and wash my hands of the whole thing."

"You must think I'm a fool."

As indeed he was, Cavalli thought. He wondered how much Raven really knew or suspected about the Cupid and about how he himself had come by it, whether he had ever even heard of Alceo Dossena. He wondered too how soon d'Espinal would tell him, or if he would at all. Since d'Espinal appeared to be a rogue himself, that was doubtful, he decided, and said, "Let us talk about your Mr. Harcourt d'Espinal. Who has today gone to Rome, to call on Niccolò Sabbioni." He leaned back in his chair, smiling, and told Raven carefully all that he had gleaned about d'Espinal's activities. "So there you have it," he finished. "The man is a fraud, and he will almost certainly cheat you. What is the word? Double-cross."

"Have you evidence of that?" Raven asked.

"Not precisely—not yet. But I expect to have, by the day after tomorrow." To his surprise Raven started to laugh, not his habitual bleakness but with real amusement, and Cavalli gazed at him disapprovingly. "I do not appreciate the joke."

"No?" Raven dabbed his lips with a handkerchief.

"Not even with your scheming mind? The sooner you get that evidence the better. If it's true, d'Espinal is just the man we need."

"I do not see how. Not even with my subtle mind."

"My dear Bruno." Raven was rarely so friendly, and Cavalli grew cautious. "Let him handle the deal. But now if anything goes wrong we lose nothing. If he brings it off and gets Polliano to your ceremony in the bank, all we have to say is, 'Thank you for your efforts, Mr. d'Espinal, and good day to you.' He's in no position to make terms, and you'll still get your third share." Raven laughed again. "We can kick this Isola San Giorgio Piccolo from under his feet. Given the proof, his dear friend Mrs. Messina-Silvestro will see him run out of Venice, and these two women with him."

That should appeal to his damned Roman mania for intrigue, Raven thought, and Cavalli nodded judicially. "Yes. That is quite good. I feel we might have something here. And, let me point out, entirely due to my work."

"Of course," the colonel agreed. "Anything you like. But now you can produce the Cupid again, from wherever it is."

It was his turn to smile at Raven again. "Only when the deal is settled, at the Bank of America and Italy."

Raven started something but then stopped and sat drumming lightly with his fingertips on the desk, thinking that it would be quite possible to feel almost affectionate about anyone who chose to murder this little man. But he said, "It doesn't matter. If d'Espinal's gone to see Sabbioni, we can presume he's interested." And suspicious, Cavalli thought, but he said nothing, and Raven asked, "What if he also happens to hear something about Polliano's background?"

Cavalli shrugged. "I have no idea how big a fool he is. He might decide he has healthier interests."

"He might indeed. So we leave him no choice. What you must do is to call Polliano yourself. Tell him that the arrangements are taking too long and you have to leave on more urgent business. If he wishes to go further now he must contact Signor Harcourt d'Espinal on Isola San Giorgio Piccolo."

"I get more than tired of being told what I must do," Cavalli complained. "Yet the idea is appealing, and certainly safer for me. But what do you hope to achieve?"

"To have him involved, whether he likes it or not. Then with your story of his business methods I can give him his instructions. Once committed I don't think d'Espinal will have any fixations about stopping at half a million. He knows what the Cupid's worth."

"One hopes you may be right." Cavalli seemed to be amused again. Being in the trade himself, Signor d'Espinal would almost certainly know what the thing was worth. About one thousand dollars. He said, "It's almost genius, Colonel Raven. And you tell me that I have a scheming mind."

D'Espinal booked in at the Hassler-Villa Medici on the Piazza Trinità dei Monti at the top of the Spanish Steps. Damnably expensive, but one should never overlook the value of a good address, especially in Rome; nor the importance of coolness and elevation in the noisiest, certainly the most sophisticated—and today apparently the hottest—city in the world. He lost no time in having the exquisite young gentleman in reception make a telephone call for him, then taking it in the privacy of his own suite. This perhaps was the most uncertain moment; if that ancient rascal refused to meet him at such short notice he might waste a great deal of time. But one did not think he would, not if one used a certain nice diplomacy. In fact the curious, sweetly acid voice which answered did say at first, "A thousand pardons, signore, but the maestro does not receive without an appointment. And that only after several days."

"Dear me," d'Espinal murmured. "I have so little time in Rome. Perhaps you should mention my name once more. And be so exquisitely kind as to mention also a silver-gilt Cellini saltcellar now in the possession of the Marchesa dei Colti." The voice became slightly more acid still, and d'Espinal said softly, "I feel sure the maestro would wish you to mention that."

It was a longer wait then, and d'Espinal sat by the window gazing out over the glittering panorama of Rome: three civilizations superimposed upon each other, he reflected, and the last one probably the worst. Red-tiled rooftops and gleaming spires and steeples, a fantasy in terra cotta and ocher, brown and white and pink, with the great dome of Saint Peter's brooding over it all in a golden haze. Every city had its own atmospheric color, he thought: Venice opalescent blue and Rome gold. That the gold was largely dust raised by the maniacal traffic and the crowds on the teeming streets below did not detract in the least from its beauty.

The telephone whispered, *"Pronto,"* and there was a faint note of surprise in it this time. It said, "The maestro asks me also to mention a certain Ghirlandaio cartoon in the possession of Mrs. Messina-Silvestro of Venice."

D'Espinal's eyes opened a fraction wider. So that monumental woman had been doubtful. She had sent dear Emilia's delightful little drawing out for examination after all; and apparently the old rascal had authenticated it, so what was he about now? D'Espinal said, "The maestro is exceedingly well informed. To be precise, my dear friend, Mrs. Messina-Silvestro has herself now sold the Ghirlandaio. Was there any other message?"

"The maestro will receive you at five o'clock this afternoon. For exactly thirty minutes."

A papal audience, d'Espinal thought, but he said, "A thousand thanks. I shall hasten to present myself."

He hung up smiling and thinking what a clever old rascal it was, took the elevator to the roof-garden restaurant for lunch and sat there gazing down benevolently at the gracious architectural curves of the Spanish Steps far below with the massed color of their traditional flower sellers seated at the foot of them.

Angela herself was high up on a roof too, over the old palace. A secret corner she had discovered one day when trying to befriend a kitten, following it up flight after flight of steps and out through a surprising doorway onto the leads. The panorama of rooftops and towers and domes enchanted her; it was the only place she knew in Venice where you could be quite sure of drowsing lazily in the shade without being disturbed, and she had a great deal to think about quietly today.

If that baby was made of stone, she thought, it must be a statue. It was called the Cupid and it must be important because clearly those two men wanted it; Signor d'Espinal had even gone to Rome to see about it and Signor Cavalli was afraid for it. He had told her so much himself in his whispering. Therefore he would not have dropped it into the lagoon, he would have taken it somewhere to hide. And when one remembered his vanishing on the San Niccolò road, then coming back again looking pleased, it was quite easy to guess where that must be: the old graveyard. It was a good place for a statue. So one could rest now, during the heat.

Sleeping curled up like a cat, she woke and stretched when the clocks all round boomed out four. Carefully finishing the chicken first, she counted her money—now two thousand four hundred and fifty lire—tied on her sandals, hoping that they would stand up to another long walk, and picked her way down to the campo. It was still quiet and deserted, and she glanced back once at Cavalli's balcony and then set off deliberately for San Zaccaria and the Lido ferry. In less than another hour she was plodding along the wide, empty road beside the lagoon on the Lido.

Once out past the hotels there was nothing except an occasional automobile, and she went on until the big church came into view, still flaring red in the sunshine. This was the place where Signor Cavalli had vanished and where she herself had discovered that rusted gate behind the trees with its sad old dark-green graveyard beyond. But before going in she set out to search along the lagoon side, where the water lapped up to the long grass. There, almost at once, she found the mark of a boat in the mud. It could have been any boat, of course, but she was convinced it was Mario's. It was nearly opposite the gate, and she felt sure this was where the signore had come at one o'clock last night. Satisfied then, she turned back across the road.

She hesitated here, but she could not stop now after coming so far, and with a last look back at the sunlit lagoon she edged through the opening. Surprisingly it was not so frightening once inside, even peaceful and friendly in a strange, drowsy way. With her natural curiosity taking hold, yet still moving silently as if careful of waking someone, she crept from one tombstone to another puzzling over the inscriptions —of a kind she had never seen before—growing bolder gradually and exploring one overgrown path after another. But there was no sign of the Cupid.

In the end she found it by accident. She was about to turn back, bitterly disappointed, when a hanging branch of some thorny tree swept off her hat and, bending down to retrieve it, she discovered one last flat slab against a ruined old brick wall, almost completely hidden by a soft, trailing shrub. The Cupid was lying on that as naturally as if it had been there forever, looking as old as the cemetery itself and actually part of the tombstone. Only when she put out her hand tentatively, finding that it moved a little, did she realize that this must really be Signor Cavalli's baby. Then she sat down on her heels to study it.

It was really rather disappointing, not very much after all, she decided, and she certainly could not imagine why anyone should want it so badly or why the signore should make so much fuss over it. It did not even look like a very nice baby. With an expression like that on its face, you would say it was going to get into mischief at any time. But she had a sudden feeling that she ought to be careful now. It was useful to know where the Cupid was—she might make even more money out of it yet. But it must be dangerous for Signor Cavalli to hide it like this, and until she knew why, it would be best to say nothing about it to anyone, not even Signor d'Espinal. That was another lesson she had learned in Chioggia: it was always wise to keep one's own secrets.

At last she let the creeper fall back and, with her hat the only splash of color in the dim greenness, went out into the sunlight on the road again, while at the same time and barely half a mile away, a big black Mercedes was taking the bend by the church and opening up on the long Riviera San Niccolò towards the ancient graveyard.

They had brought the automobile from Rome because, surprisingly, Alberto was a fast and skillful driver and Polliano often liked to take a ride in the afternoons; he said it made his stomach feel better. Today he had taken a fit to have them go all round the Lido, heading east along the Adriatic beach, turning at the Porto di Lido past the airport and coming back by the Riviera on the northern side. It was a good enough drive, though Alberto, irritated by Polly continually telling him to take it easy, considered that when you had done it once you had done it forever, and this was the third time, while Ricci thought simply that it was just goddamned monotonous; he thought they were going to have a showdown with

Polly anytime soon. And then Alberto said, "Well, whaddaya know."

The bright hat was unmistakable as Angela slipped out from the trees on the left, crossed over unconcernedly to the waterside and started back towards the town with her back to them.

"What now?" Polliano asked irritably. "It's only a kid."

"It's that kid," Ricci grunted. "She tailed us after this guy Cavalli. I'd say she knows something—and maybe too much. Seems kinda funny that wherever we are that kid comes in."

Alberto slowed down carefully. "That kid's trouble. You want I should pick her up?"

"God's sake, what do I want with kids?" Polliano demanded. "Run her off the road if that's the way you feel."

Alberto nodded. Never very clear about his own motivations, he probably did not quite realize why he did it himself. Perhaps some obscure premonition, perhaps just the temptation of that small, lonely figure walking doggedly along the long, deserted road. He put his foot down hard.

The Mercedes was on Angela almost before she knew it was there. A rasp of tires on the grit and she swung round for one instant to see the shining black monster seeming almost to spring at her. She was never quite to know how she saved herself, whether she was actually thrown clear or whether she leapt aside. But she caught her own despairing wail, felt herself falling over the four-foot bank and clutching at the long grass with her feet in the water, felt the hot wind from the automobile as it swept past.

Half dazed, she heard it skid to a stop, footsteps

coming back, and she crouched in the grass like a small, terrified animal. Then they were standing above her, the two she most feared and another, a tall, thin gray man. They looked down at her, and she was too frightened even to scream, but somehow she found her voice, feeling sick. She whispered, "Please, I know where it is—the baby. Please to let me go and I'll show you." She was crying again.

Alberto took a step forward, saying over his shoulder, "What did I tell you? We got to—" But Ricci was watching back along the road, the way they had come, and he cut in sharply, "Hold it."

Angela risked one quick look sideways. It was a carabinieri patrol jeep roaring up fast, stopping with a screech, and one of the men leaning out: a lieutenant. He asked, "What is it here?"

Just for an instant Angela knew the three of them were worried. They were afraid, and it was the thin one who answered, "Why nothing, not much. I guess we scared this poor kid. She sorta jumped over the edge. Maybe we were going too fast." He added, "We're at the Ludovico Manin."

"You were," the lieutenant agreed, "much too fast." He got down, taking them all in, the Mercedes and Angela's pale, tear-stained face. "Is she hurt?" They had been too far away, just rounding the bend themselves, to see what had really happened, but these people looked reliable enough and one did not like to upset tourists—particularly tourists in the Mercedes and Ludovico Manin class. "Get up," he told Angela.

She crept out, clutching her hat, wondering desperately whether she dare run, even whether she could, and Polliano turned his curious sweet smile on her. "There don't seem to be much damage, kid." Suddenly he was holding out a big brown note, five thousand lire, saying, "Here. Maybe that'll help to make it better." He looked at the lieutenant. "D'you need us to stick around?"

They walked back to the Mercedes, the lieutenant watching them as they drove off, still not quite satisfied; it might be worthwhile checking at the Manin to see who they were. But there was no reason on earth why they should try to kill this solemn little waif. You got some crazy characters on the Lido sometimes but not as crazy as that. Nevertheless he asked, "Did they run you down?"

Angela was recovering quickly. This *carabiniere* looked like a nice man, but the less one had to do with police the better; there would be endless questions if nothing worse, so she said, "No, signore, truly. I was walking in the grass and then I saw something shining on the road and I thought it might be a hundred-lire piece and stepped out. Then the automobile was there."

The little devil was lying, he thought. She had probably been standing by the side of the road with her hand out and those characters had driven past too close, to frighten her a bit. He asked, "Where are you going?"

That frightened her again. "To visit a very good friend of mine," she told him. "A very good man. He keeps the *gelati* bar on the corner of the Via Negroponte."

The lieutenant nodded. "Luigi Battista. Well, I know him at least. Just see you don't go looking for any more hundred-lire pieces on the way, or you might not get there. And don't go spending all that money on ice cream."

He climbed back into the jeep, and Angela watched it roar away, keeping carefully to the edge of the road. She was quite certain that those men really had tried to hit her, but equally there was no doubt that Sant' Anna was also looking after her personally, so everything would work out in the end, and in the meantime she had another five thousand lire. Now she could certainly afford to go to Luigi Battista's bar and buy a Coca-Cola—although one still ought not to be extravagant.

Chapter Six

When the afternoon heat had cooled a little d'Espinal walked majestically along the Via Sistina in the pleasant shade of its tall, late-Renaissance buildings, dull ocher and pale terra cotta against the coppery-blue sky. It was a little eccentric to walk perhaps but, as much at home here as he was in Florence and Paris, Munich and London—indeed, it was here and in Florence that he had first started to acquire his abiding love and very wide knowledge of Italian art— he always said that the only real way to understand Rome was through the soles of your feet. He emerged into the roar and bustle and light of the Piazza Barberini, reflecting on the splendid vitality with which these Roman drivers imagined they were still racing in the Circus Maximus, turned left, and left again, into the Via Vittoria Veneto.

He could have come here more directly too. Old Sabbioni's apartment was up at the most elegant end, near the Pinciana Gate and the Borghese Gardens, but he liked to stroll the length of this street: American on one side, Italian the other. Rows of blue sunshades and tables, banks of flowers and expensive establishments, idling, gossiping crowds; more elegant than the Viale Elisabetta in Venice and more than a rival to the Champs Elysées.

D'Espinal was not quite sure at first whether it was

a boy or girl who opened the double doors to him at the head of a beautiful but now rather dilapidated marble staircase. Long golden-brown hair, a flowing white silk shirt and tight black velvet trousers, a petulant face and the same sweetly acid voice as on the telephone, faintly spiteful. It said, "Please to wait, signore." He was left alone in what had once been a handsome reception hall but now, like the staircase, showed traces of neglect: a heavy atmosphere, the tiled floor slightly dull, a few quite fair pictures glowing softly on the walls but not up to the standard one would have expected of Sabbioni and, more indicative still, several telltale spaces where others had obviously been removed. "So," d'Espinal murmured, "the old rascal has been selling off his collection."

When the boy took him in—it was a boy, d'Espinal decided, a sort of decadent and probably vicious pre-Raphaelite angel, a sick style he had never cared for —Sabbioni was sitting at a tall window overlooking the three great arches of the gate and the gardens beyond. The room also had an indefinable air of neglect: two or three fair pictures, but by no means remarkable; a pair of painted Faenza plates and a gilded Campagna statuette set in a niche on a black marble pedestal, which was at once too wide and too low for it; and a faded, signed photograph of Benito Mussolini.

The old man appeared to have been dozing lightly, but he blinked his eyes open and murmured, "Sit there," and then sat without speaking himself, watching d'Espinal. In a way not unlike Paolo Raffaele, he thought, but incredibly more ancient: a light shawl over his shoulders in spite of the heat, paper-thin fingers resting on the arms of his chair and a floss of soft white hair. You would have said an elderly scholar waiting quietly to die, except for the eyes— and they were alert and malicious, even at this moment faintly amused. At last he whispered, "You sent me an impertinent message. Some nonsense about a Benvenuto Cellini saltcellar."

"Not impertinent, maestro," d'Espinal protested. "One would never be that. I happened to observe it in the Colti Collection, and the Marchesa, it appears, acquired it through you. It was made in Munich. By one Jakob Harsch—about four years ago. A superb craftsman. The dear fellow offered it to me at one time." He looked down his nose modestly. "I felt my own reputation was perhaps too slender to sustain it." There was another long silence until he added, "And you, maestro, mentioned something about a Ghirlandaio cartoon."

Sabbioni was laughing, although it was barely audible. "We might talk about that some other day. What do you want?"

"I imagine Mrs. Messina-Silvestro sent it to you for authentication. I myself classified it as being possible, but perhaps slightly dubious. What a remarkable woman she is. Did you ever hear that when her late husband lay dying he said she should be preserved in the Vatican archives?"

"The woman's a self-important fool, and I gave her the answer she expected. I don't imagine you came here to talk about Mrs. Messina-Silvestro."

"It was you who brought the subject up, maestro.

Like most people, I would prefer not to. Except to admit myself gratefully in your debt. Your report greatly enhanced my reputation with the dear lady."

"That can easily be broken again."

"And your Cellini saltcellar with the Marchesa dei Colti?" d'Espinal asked. "Need we talk about such distressing things?"

"I'm waiting to hear what you do want to talk about, Mr. d'Espinal."

"Then I shall tell you." D'Espinal smiled at him benevolently. "There are some curious rumors afloat in Venice—along the canals, as it were. They have led me into undertaking a little light, entertaining research. Into the life and works and friends of Alceo Dossena, about 1918 to 1928. The name must be familiar to you."

If one who was already so still could become even more immobile, Sabbioni seemed to do so; he looked, d'Espinal thought, like some kind of ancient, guarded serpent. One could not hope to get any direct answers, of course, but there was much to be gained merely by watching his reactions; it was all one had come here for and it would be enough. The old man seemed to be listening to the noise floating up from the street, the indescribable babel of Rome, before he asked, "Well?"

"Three questions in particular," d'Espinal said. "The answers would be most instructive. You would be in your thirties then, maestro, already laying the foundations of an enviable career. Did you ever meet Dossena himself? Did your most respected father, Giulio Sabbioni, as a great dealer in antique statuary, ever give or sell to Dossena a massive but probably comparatively worthless work in marble of the late fifteenth century? And did you ever know an Alfredo Fasoli, a goldsmith of the Via Mario de Fiori?"

Sabbioni closed his eyes again. "I tire easily, Mr. d'Espinal. And that was fifty years ago."

"I shall not detain you long. Let me refresh your memory, maestro. That Frascati wine bar on the Via Mario, Christmas Eve 1916, the First World War, when a poor private soldier entered carrying a parcel wrapped in newspaper. He drank a glass of Chianti and presently opened the parcel up, explained that he needed money and would the barman care to buy this exquisite little Madonna carved in wood. The barman himself was not interested, but perhaps scenting a small commission, which no good Roman ever refuses, he sent for an Alfredo Fasoli, a goldsmith, from his workshop across the street. This Fasoli perceived the quality of the work at once and gave Dossena one hundred lire for it—worth rather more then, of course, than it is now."

"Should this interest me?" the old man asked.

"I think so," d'Espinal told him. "May I continue? It was only when Fasoli came to examine the Madonna more closely that he saw it was of quite recent workmanship, but most skillfully aged. He then began to think that the hands which had produced this little masterpiece might produce others, and he made it his business to seek out Dossena and put certain proposals to him. In short, it was Fasoli who set up Dossena in a studio workshop near the Castel Sant' Angelo on his discharge from military service in 1918. It was Fasoli who started Dossena on his extraordinary career. Which ended in one of the greatest artistic scandals of recent times and shook the reputations of some of the world's greatest experts."

"It's all so long ago, Mr. d'Espinal. It's an old story."

"Not really, maestro. One might even say the story continues. There is some reason to believe that a previously unknown work by Dossena has suddenly appeared in Venice. There is a rumor that it is being offered as a Michelangelo. At one million dollars." D'Espinal smiled gently. "While as a Dossena it is worth at best one thousand. On my information it is to be sold to a person named Polliano. A rather simple fellow, I feel. But I suspect that he would be most intrigued and amused if he were told what it really is, what it is really worth."

Sabbioni appeared to be asleep. It was a long minute before he answered. "One imagines he would be. I wonder if Mrs. Messina-Silvestro would be equally intrigued and amused if she were informed that on later consideration her Ghirlandaio cartoon is undoubtedly a forgery?"

"You know, I don't think so," d'Espinal said. "I really don't, maestro. She might even be quite annoyed. Our good lady has already sold the Ghirlandaio and she might even regard the suggestion as casting some doubt on her own integrity. Whereas my dear friend the Marchesa still treasures her Cellini salt-cellar. And old Jakob Harsch would be quite willing to swear that he sold it to you in all good faith as a reproduction."

The old man nodded slowly. "You are a clever man, Mr. d'Espinal. And sometimes unpleasant things happen to clever men. I could find it possible to wish that something inexpressibly unpleasant might happen to you."

"Come now, maestro," d'Espinal begged. "Let us not be unchristian. I had even hoped that some day we might arrange some business together ourselves. I have several entertaining little projects in mind." There was a definite spark of interest in the ancient rascal's eyes, d'Espinal thought. He said, "But for the present . . ."

He repeated his three questions clearly and carefully, and Niccolò Sabbioni nodded again, rather drowsily. "I want to sleep," he complained. "But I see there'll be no peace until I tell you. I did know Fasoli. And Alceo Dossena, of course. And my father did sell him a marble, an unfinished thing, fifteenth century— a mess. Some clumsy brute of an apprentice had hacked it about since then. There was a crack in it and Dossena actually used that . . ." He chuckled softly. "By God, he was a clever boy. We'd have made his fortune for him if he'd waited a little longer." Sabbioni's voice trailed off into a faint snore, but then he jerked awake, blinking at d'Espinal again. He said distinctly, "Don't try anything with Polliano, Mr. d'Espinal. He's a bad one, that, an ugly animal. Now let me be, will you? I'm tired."

The pretty, spiteful boy was waiting in the hall, the place heavy with heat and silence, and d'Espinal thought suddenly of the clear, light space of San Giorgio, Mrs. Teestock serving English afternoon tea and the cool, perhaps even rather hard, poise of Emilia. But there was still something he wanted, if it was to be had, and he accepted his hat, saying, "The maestro is growing very frail," and taking out a five thousand note. He asked, "Would you be insulted by a small appreciation?"

"Who ever is?" the boy inquired.

"Who indeed," d'Espinal murmured, "especially in Rome?" He glanced around the hall. "It appears the maestro is disposing of some of his collection. The charming little Campagna statuette in his room. Was there ever anything else exhibited on that pedestal?" The pre-Raphaelite angel did not answer, and d'Espinal sighed gently and took out another note to go with the first. "A reclining child?" he suggested. "A cupid?"

Almost imperceptibly the boy nodded and d'Espinal breathed, "Ah . . . and how long since it disappeared?"

Eyeing the notes, he said, "Perhaps six, seven months."

D'Espinal nodded. Going down the sweeping, once-beautiful staircase, he thought it was little enough for ten thousand—only the confirmation of something which he knew must be the only possible answer. But one liked to have everything clear.

Emerging into the restless brilliance of the Via Veneto, he paused again. All Rome was out now, sitting at the tables under their sunshades, gossiping, intriguing, studying the women, watching the old *carrozzas* clopping past, and he could not very well walk on without stopping for a few minutes at the Café de Paris to watch the spectacle himself. It would be pleasant to have Emilia here now. Emilia would become so much a part of this, he thought, and then frowned slightly. Emilia could easily become a small problem; it was important to remember that Emilia was only a business associate. For the present he was not dissatisfied. Two or three telephone calls, mostly about this fellow Polliano, and he could return to Venice with a fairly complete picture. And a picture by no means unamusing. He hoped to make it more amusing still before he was done with it.

In Venice too Bruno Cavalli was thinking much the same. He hung up the telephone telling himself that it was a crazy scheme, but if it pleased that damned colonel it did no harm either, and it was certainly entertaining to set the fat Englishman to taking chestnuts out of the fire for them both. At the same time, in their gilt-and-yellow suite in the Ludovico Manin, Icarus Polliano replaced the receiver with a look on his face which startled even Ricci. He asked, "What now, Polly?"

Polliano sat down painfully in one of the spindly little satin armchairs. He said, "What now is that goddamned Signor Cavalli . . ." He added a vividly descriptive phrase in Sicilian argot. "Cavalli claims he is pulling out. He claims the whole deal is now turned over to some Limey named d'Espinal." He tripped over the name himself. "I think I got it right. D'Espinal, on someplace called Isola San Giorgio Piccolo. And right now this d'Espinal's in Rome, but he comes back tomorrow, maybe the day after. And he's a tough dealer, so it could be the price goes up again. So what d'you work out on that?"

"What I worked out all along," Ricci told him. "That they've been taking you for a monkey."

"That's right, Ricci," Polliano agreed. "So when did you ever know anybody try that and get away with it?" He looked across at Alberto idly riffling through a pack of cards, playing some incomprehensible, solitary game of his own, and added, "Okay, if that's what they want."

"So we get some action?" Alberto asked.

"So we pull out," Ricci grunted. "Hell with it, Polly, this goddamned stone baby ain't worth the trouble. We made a bad break this afternoon—that kid and the cop."

Alberto poured himself a long bourbon. "You getting soft too, Ricci? I keep telling you that kid's trouble. And she knows something."

"We pull out when I say," Polliano told Ricci softly. "The cop don't signify. He was happy enough. And 'Berto could be right about the kid at that. As for the baby . . ." He pushed his lower lip out slightly, and Alberto thought it looked like Polly was getting back to the old days, like he used to be. "Okay, maybe it was a sick fancy. I'd have given ten, fifteen grand, but maybe I don't want it any more. It was just a kind of interest. Except I mean to have it now, just to show folks don't take me for a sucker. D'you recollect Luciano and that parcel of snow, Ricci? What was he asking for it—two million bucks? And what did he get? D'you remember?"

"Sure," Ricci said expressionlessly. "I remember." He had every reason to; he had shot Luciano himself.

"Maybe we been a trifle easygoing, but nobody's

getting soft." Polliano turned his sad, sweet smile on both of them. "Could be 'Berto's right about this kid. So you locate her first. Maybe she does know where the baby is—that's what she said. So we beat it out of her, and how she fits in. That fills out tomorrow. If the kid's no good after all, we go visit this d'Espinal day after. And if it's no dice there either you can stop by on Signor Smart-Guy Cavalli and kinda close the deal. We don't have to hurry. I'd say we leave for Rome ourselves on Sunday. Now for God's sake let's relax," he finished irritably. "You'll set my guts off again, and I got a poker game set up tonight."

Alberto finished his bourbon and shook his head. "I don't go so good with poker lately. And that kid sorta worries me. I reckon she comes from Venice, so she goes back there. I reckon I'll go watch the ferry for a time.

From that evening to the next, when she met d'Espinal at the air terminal, Angela never knew how many escapes she had. She spent it washing up for Luigi Battista in his bar. After the hot day there was a constant stream of customers coming back from the bathing beach to the ferry, and Luigi was glad of the help, though wondering privately what one ought to do about this homeless little waif, and they were too busy to talk much. At one point Alberto actually walked past and saw her there, although she did not see him. And then the lieutenant of *carabinieri* came in. He was in civilian clothes and had two children with him, beautifully dressed children, Angela thought enviously, so they were probably only out for an evening walk. But she noticed that he glanced at her, and while the two children were eating their *gelati* at one of the tables outside, he stood talking to Luigi and looking back at her.

Angela made up her mind quickly. Luigi was a good, kind man but, like the woman at the other café-bar where she sometimes worked, he might easily have this idea of handing her over to the police. She dried the last glass carefully, placed it on the shelf and hung up the towel, took her hat just as they were coming in through the doorway. And as she quite expected, the lieutenant asked, "Well, little girl, don't you think we ought to do something about you?"

Glancing wildly along the hundred yards or so to the ferry, she said, "Please, signore, I must go now. My mama and papa will wonder where I am." A moment later she was running up the avenue. She stopped at the corner to look back, but neither of them seemed to be following, and she crossed over the wide *piazzale* to the ferry station.

Again she did not see Alberto, but he watched the bright hat flash past and followed more slowly; he was in no hurry. Like they did with Cavalli, he could take a taxi and be waiting for the little bastard at San Zaccaria. But Angela went on to one of the smaller water-buses this time—much cheaper than the big ferry and it actually called at the Exposition Gardens, quite near her hut. Neither did she notice the taxi roaring past while she stood in the overcrowded boat and thanked Sant' Anna once more. So as Alberto waited uselessly at the main waterfront, she was loitering in the noisy, lively working quarter of the Via Garibaldi half a mile away, listening to the cheerful Italian gossip, buying a pizza and sitting down in the corner of a doorway to eat it complacently. She could not guess how dangerous Alberto was becoming. This kid was getting to be a personal thing with him, an insult, almost a superstition.

When d'Espinal stepped ashore from the airport launch that next evening he was surprised and, so far as it was possible with him, even a little irritated to find Angela waiting. But the child looked alarmed, even more pinched than usual, and he inquired kindly enough, "Why, Angela Caterina, what are you doing here? Did Signorina Annunzietta send you to meet me?"

"If you please," she started nervously, "I had other business." She looked back over her shoulder and asked, "But could I come back to your island now?"

There was no doubt she was frightened, though he could not see anything particularly strange in the usual crowd milling about the building. But Angela knew that Ricci and Alberto were there. She had been dodging them all day, from the time they had first seen her in Saint Mark's Square that morning to the afternoon, when she had crept down from her hiding place on the roof of the old palace to find them waiting in the Campo Sant' Anna. She had just escaped them by running wildly, and only since then by keeping as close as she dared to the two *carabinieri* who were always on duty at the terminal. That had been a double terror.

But in the way Signor d'Espinal seemed to have of commanding everything, a taxi appeared at the steps immediately. She just had time to see Ricci and Alberto walking off fast, and in a minute more they themselves were skimming away past the palace. Sitting in the other armchair—looking a little too large for it, Angela thought—he asked suddenly, "Well, Angela Caterina, are you still hungry? And why are you so nervous? Have you been about some small prank?"

"I am nearly always hungry," she admitted. "But as to being nervous . . ." She stopped. She was not clear what prank was, but he really seemed to be looking at her very strangely, and one still had to be careful. She said, "I did not like the *carabinieri*. People say they would shut me up in the Old Prison over the Bridge of Sighs. Or send me back to . . ."—she stopped again—"where I come from. And I don't want to go."

To live in such a world of imaginary fears, poor child, he thought. He said, "I'm afraid you'll have to, you know. We shall have to find out where your home is."

It was just possible that sooner or later she might have told d'Espinal everything; several times already today she had half decided she would. Yet now it appeared that he was like all the rest of them, though not so bad as those other men, of course; he would not try to kill her, but being sent back to Chioggia was nearly as bad, especially when she was doing so well. She sighed gently. She just had to depend upon herself and Sant' Anna, remember what Signor Cavalli had sent her here for and that there was another five thousand lire in it. That was one more thing her aunt's new husband often remarked: "Never open your mouth until you see a profit to bite at." Well, she wouldn't, but for the present it was something to take a taxi ride like this, flying into the blue on clouds of spray.

At first sight too the island was enchanting, a garden and a pink house, a tower and cypress trees all glowing softly in the setting sun; but what followed next was not so pleasant. Signor d'Espinal simply turned her over to an impossibly superior girl older than herself, named Graziella, who turned out to be the maid, and a fat woman he called Mrs. Pietro, saying they would look after her. In fact they did not seem to like her very much. They both made a fuss about her clothes, took them away from her to be washed, with an argument about the money she had in her pocket, and hustled her off to take a bath. It was true they gave her another meal afterwards, but they asked a great many questions—where had she got all that money from and the hat—and when she would not tell them, Mrs. Pietro announced flatly that she was mulish. Lying in bed afterwards, much earlier than she usually went, Angela thought bitterly that she did not like this place at all, and obviously the less one said here about anything the better. They would not even let her see Signor d'Espinal again; they said it was not her place to go and bother him.

She fell asleep thinking it could be dangerous here too. It was a very lonely place, and those two men had seen her getting into the taxi with Signor d'Espinal. They must know where she was, and they could easily come to fetch her.

That at least she need not have worried about—for the present. Ricci and Alberto had worked it out, although they had never seen d'Espinal before nor he them yet. They had said that nobody but a Limey could look like that, so it must be this guy and he must have taken the kid to this San Giorgio place. Smarting with the frustration of having her slip through their fingers all day, Alberto wanted to go and get her right now. But Polliano was still showing them who gave the orders. He said, "Okay. So we know where she is, so we stick to schedule." Polly always believed in sticking to schedule.

Chapter Seven

It was good to find her clothes so fresh and clean in the morning and to have breakfast in the kitchen. There were Mrs. Pietro and Graziella and two other girls who came over from San Francesco to help in the house. They asked her a great many questions, and Mrs. Pietro said she was mulish again, but she learned a lot too. That the padrona's husband had been a soldier and the padrona herself had been here for twenty years or more and Signorina Pentecost had come from Paris tired and ill five, six years ago. Sometimes the signorina had been a little difficult, but she was a different person since Signor d'Espinal arrived last summer. They did not know why he had first come, but Mrs. Pietro said it was a business matter to start with, though anybody could see it was much more than that now, especially with the signorina. Anyhow, they all loved the signore. He was comic, he was kind and generous and unfailingly courteous; and he was here very often from London and Paris and other places, sometimes only for a few days or a week, sometimes for a month or more.

Then it was not so good when Mrs. Pietro made her help with the work. Even worse when just before lunch Graziella announced, "They are here," and she was taken through to a large, beautiful room where there was a grand piano, elegant furniture and big windows opening out into the garden. The signore was there with the padrona—a rather elderly brownish-gray lady who looked somehow like a mother superior, though of course wearing different and not very becoming clothes—and Signorina Pentecost. She really was rather beautiful, Angela decided, dressed in a soft green linen dress, dark hair and eyes, and a quiet sort of face which changed completely when she smiled. Angela felt she might take to Signorina Pentecost, but Mrs. Teestock was more like a mother superior than ever when she started asking questions, and so many of them. It was not really very successful, and at last the signorina suggested gently, "Perhaps Angela will tell us more about herself when she's settled down."

"I'm afraid you'll have to," Mrs. Teestock told her. "You'll have to tell us where you come from, my dear."

"I'll take her back to Mrs. Pietro," Emilia interrupted. I expect it's all a little overwhelming at first."

Privately d'Espinal considered that Mrs. Teestock was being a trifle too efficient and institutional with the child, though she certainly could be a singularly unengaging little creature if she chose. When Emilia came back she said, "Poor Angela. She is rather mysterious, and Mrs. Pietro's very suspicious. It appears she's got over six thousand lire on her. She says she's been saving it to buy new sandals, but Mrs. Pietro wants to know where it came from. And she does seem to be very inquisitive."

"Curiosity is a prerogative of the young, my dear," d'Espinal reminded her. "Though the six thousand lire is somewhat curious. But I have already observed that she seems to have a highly developed business sense."

"More likely to be highly developed fingers," Mrs. Teestock answered tartly. "However, we must do our best for her. We must have a good talk this afternoon. She certainly needs new sandals—new clothes altogether. I shall take her to Venice tomorrow to get them. And, of course, take her to the police." With an air of moving on to more important things she announced, "I think I should like a glass of sherry before lunch," and asked, "Now, Harcourt, what did you discover in Rome?"

D'Espinal contrived to look both complacent and mysterious. "Enough to piece together a not unamusing picture. And some moderately startling information about this fellow Polliano. One now sees through a glass a little less darkly. But yourselves first. How did you fare?"

"I hope it is amusing." Emilia took out and lit a cigarette carefully. "I still don't like this, Harry. I have a feeling we might be starting something we can't stop, and I enjoy this life. I don't want to spoil it." She glanced across at d'Espinal.

Mrs. Teestock made a sound which from any other than an English country lady might have been interpreted as a hearty snort, and said, "First, Harcourt, your Colonel Raven. We talked to Clara Messina-Silvestro. It's quite appalling how much of other people's business that woman knows. Colonel Raven took that house in the Calle della Pietà about four months ago. He is engaged on a new biography of Benito Mussolini, from a rather more sympathetic viewpoint than most. Which endears him to Clara—she has leanings that way herself. And he is particularly interested in discovering what really happened to the Dongo treasure."

"Beautiful, dear lady," d'Espinal breathed. "Really beautiful. It establishes another link, small but significant. There is a signed photograph of Mussolini in old Sabbioni's apartment. While a concern with the treasure would account for Raven working in the Lake Como area. The Dongo treasure," he explained kindly to Emilia, "was several thousand million lire in bullion, various currencies, and supposed works of art which Benito Mussolini took with him when trying to escape into Switzerland in April 1945. It disappeared completely when he was shot at Dongo, and trying to discover exactly where it went has been an interesting speculation ever since."

"I know," Emilia told him shortly. "And I know that most of the people connected with it are now dead."

"My dear," he assured her, "I promise that the Dongo treasure has nothing to do with our Cupid. Or rather it is only the background. As one might say, the germ of the idea. What an ingenious old rogue Sabbioni is. And the good Father Rossi, of 1720?" he asked.

"Most illuminating," Mrs. Teestock said. "The present priest was not at first all that forthcoming, but I happened to mention that I am something of an authority on altar cloths, and it would give me great pleasure to design and embroider one for him, though I really don't know when I shall find time to fit it in.

After that we got on famously. He could not show us enough. There are old church records in Father Rossi's handwriting. And there was a person who asked permission to photograph them, some four or five months ago."

"Not Colonel Raven?"

"An Italian. A smallish, plump man who claimed to be an historian. The priest was rather flattered. Nobody had ever considered his church worth attention before. It isn't."

"We do most excellently well," d'Espinal approved. "Pray continue."

"Domenico Galli was not so easy. He is dead. Quite naturally, in July. As you suggested, he was a very old man. And apparently a very unpleasant one. Here Emilia did sterling work. We found one of his daughters-in-law, and Emilia produced a really charming sketch portrait of the youngest child."

"A pretty little creature," Emilia murmured.

"That again," Mrs. Teestock conceded graciously, "was most effective. Briefly, Domenico Galli lived alone at a poor place some distance out of Garzeno. The daughter-in-law obviously detested him, but she had never heard of a small statue, hidden or otherwise, about the farm. Neither had her husband, his son, which was much more conclusive. What they did find when Galli died was nearly half a million lire in notes, hidden in a tin box under his bed, with written instructions that the entire sum was to be devoted to funeral expenses and masses. The woman seemed to consider that an unpardonable extravagance."

"It fits together," d'Espinal said. "And Raven himself?"

"Very little. We did not quite know where to inquire. However, we came across one old man who could have been describing him: as an inquisitive fellow asking questions about things which were best forgotten. And another who spoke of a foreigner arguing or bargaining with Galli outside the farm one day. But that's all, I'm afraid. Now, Harcourt, what did you find out?"

"The whole story—or the greater part of it. I called on Sabbioni first. A nice exercise in diplomacy, and really I fancy the old reprobate enjoyed it as much as I did myself. Sitting with his hands on the arms of a great carved chair and gazing at me like an ancient serpent, yet not without a certain malicious humor." D'Espinal described it eloquently, while Emilia watched him with a faint, rueful amusement.

"There are still certain lacunae, of course," he finished. "I still do not know the name of Sabbioni's own agent. Raven did not tell me and I did not ask Niccolò himself; I felt it was more important to establish what the Cupid really is and where it came from. I am still uncertain whether the colonel is party to the whole impudent confidence trick or whether he is quite singularly innocent. One simple question when next I meet him will probably answer that. But on your information from Mrs. Messina-Silvestro, dear lady, we can now see his original connection. Leading from that signed photograph of Benito Mussolini, I also made further inquiries elsewhere, and found that in those years before the war both Niccolò Sabbioni and his father were close to the dictator's social circle."

"So working on a sympathetic biography, Colonel Raven would naturally go to him for information?" Mrs. Teestock asked.

"Precisely. And on that I think the whole plot hinges. But for the rest, this fellow Polliano . . ." D'Espinal brooded darkly. "I felt there must be something very curious in Sabbioni's agent not wanting to deal with a million dollars in the air, and next morning I went across the river to Trastevere to find out what it was. Trastevere is the real Italian heart of Rome: there is nothing one cannot buy or sell there and nothing one cannot hear if one knows where to ask and listen. Very well, then. I asked about Polliano."

He paused, and Emilia said, "You found he doesn't have a million dollars."

D'Espinal sounded fretful. "He is thought to have a great deal more. But he also has a singularly rococo reputation. One gathers that in his heyday murder was among the more trivial of his occupations. Apparently he is now living in some circumspection, on the correct side of the law; but my informant described him as a sick old tiger who might well go hunting again merely to assure himself that he is still capable of doing so. It was a little overcolored, one felt. But they have a vivid style in Trastevere."

Emilia was really rather unseasonably amused, he thought. "And what do you expect to do about that?" she inquired gently.

"For the present," he told her, "I should like to

know what he wants the Cupid for, and exactly how and when he came into the market. One cannot avoid a suspicion that it was actually before our colonel discovered the Cupid. In short, that Niccolò Sabbioni found the customer first and then, knowing the fellow's reputation, selected an innocent to sell him the baby."

"We really must go in to lunch," Judith Teestock announced. "Mrs. Pietro will be most annoyed if we keep her waiting any longer. Does it matter what he wants it for if he's prepared to pay a million dollars?"

"Dear lady," d'Espinal said, "I don't imagine for one moment that he is."

Mrs. Teestock was beginning to find Angela Caterina very irritating. Not that she wanted children to be subservient—indeed, she disliked and distrusted them when they were—but she did expect them to appreciate it when you were trying to be helpful. She had asked Mrs. Pietro to send her to have tea with them, to have that good talk, and Angela was now sitting uncomfortably on the edge of a cane chair looking faintly dogged, with the talk dying as soon as it started. Emilia was trying to be encouraging, though with little more success, and d'Espinal was vaguely unhappy—not only on behalf of the child, but because he seemed to have introduced a sadly discordant element here.

Angela herself had a different trouble on her mind. Somehow the timing had gone wrong. This was the day she had to go and see Signor Cavalli again, at eight o'clock; she had a whole lot of things to tell him now, things she was sure he wanted to know and surely worth five thousand lire. But how could she get there? It was quite impossible. In her silent way she was almost as irritated with Mrs. Teestock as Judith with her, and after one more question and one more answer that she did not remember where she came from, except it was a long distance, she asked suddenly, "Please, may I go back to Venice?"

Mrs. Teestock was so shocked that she did not know what to say, and it was Emilia who inquired, "Why, Angela? Don't you like it here?"

"Not very . . ." Angela started, but checked herself. "Yes, indeed. It's beautiful. And your cat is very nice, and Mrs. Pietro too. But I have some important business. I have to see Signor . . ." She glanced sideways at d'Espinal and stopped again.

"You have important business, child?" Judith Teestock peered at her incredulously. There was another awkward silence before she went on, "Of course we can't keep you if you don't want to stay. But I really can't ask Mr. Pietro to get the boat out only for you. You shall go tomorrow."

The child looked so distressed that Emilia was irritated too for a moment; Judith was always so damnably firm with her good intentions. She said, "Surely you can put up with us for one more night, Angela? We'll all go tomorrow. I'll tell you what: after tea you shall come and see my studio. I'll make a drawing of you with your pretty hat." She stopped too then, looking out across the garden, and added, "I think we're having visitors. Are you expecting anyone, Judith?"

There was a boat cutting in through the afternoon haze, throwing long oily ripples away over the water and floating in the pearly blue of the lagoon and sky. It swung round to the landing steps and lay there for a few seconds before three men stepped ashore one after another. They stood there, dark figures looking at the house, and then started to move across, one walking ahead and the other two on each side of him but a pace or two behind. Somehow they seemed to be curiously purposeful, and d'Espinal noticed that the child stiffened suddenly, staring at them. Frozen quite still, clutching the edge of her chair, she was plainly terrified.

They stopped at the patio, taking in the quiet afternoon scene, and the leader asked, "It'll be Mr. Harcourt d'Espinal?"

An unpleasant-looking fellow, d'Espinal thought briefly. The gaunt face and lifeless eyes. He agreed, "I am, yes," and added formally, "You should address yourself to Mrs. Judith Teestock."

He said, "Polliano, ma'am. Icarus Polliano. And my friends Ricci Castello and 'Berto Mazzoni." Even more unpleasant, d'Espinal decided. In Trastevere he had heard them described as the gorillas, and they were looking at the girl as fixedly as she was watching them.

Mrs. Teestock inclined her head graciously. "How very kind of you to call. Do sit down. You'll take tea, of course? Angela, my dear, will you go and ask Graziella for three more cups?"

Slipping away sideways, Angela ran, her sandals flapping loudly on the flagstones under the vine pergola, Emilia looking after her and d'Espinal watching from under his eyelids. While the other two re-

mained standing—Ricci apparently faintly contemptuous and Alberto with a vague half-smile—
Polliano lowered himself onto the garden chair. Mrs.
Teestock seemed to fascinate him. He appeared to be
searching for something to say and ventured, "You
got a real nice place here, ma'am."

"It's so kind of you to say so." She smiled more
graciously than ever. "It is peaceful, we think."

"Sure." He sounded doubtful, and then snarled
suddenly, "God's sake, Ricci, 'Berto, siddown, will
you? Relax. Pardon me, ma'am," he added. "I get
irritable. I don't feel so good."

"Dear me," she said, "you're ill, Mr. Polliano?"

"Stomach, ma'am," he admitted. "You wouldn't
believe. Ulcers, so the doctors say. It gets me bad
when I'm put out. And I'm put out right now. I'm
kinda being fooled about."

"That is always unpleasant with ulcers," Judith
agreed.

"Why don't we talk?" Alberto asked. "What's with
that kid there?"

He was looking along the pergola and Polliano
snarled again. "I said to take it easy. You ain't got no
manners."

This was hovering between farce and melodrama,
d'Espinal thought, and he had a fastidious dislike of
either; it could also be damned ugly. He said, "I take
it that your call is not merely social?"

Polliano stared at him incredulously. "You mean so
it's business? Well, sure it is." He turned to Mrs.
Teestock again. "But what's with that kid, ma'am?
'Berto gets kinda interested in her."

"So are we, for that matter," Mrs. Teestock told him. "The child appears to be living as best she can in Venice and she cannot or will not tell us where she comes from or where her parents are. If she has any. Can you tell us?"

"You mean she don't have folks in Venice? She's out on her own? Well, ain't that too bad." He swiveled round to look at Alberto. "Ain't that too bad, 'Berto?"

"Mr. Polliano," d'Espinal asked, "what exactly is your business?"

"Don't you know?" He stared at d'Espinal again. "Don't Cavalli tell you?"

"And who is Cavalli?"

"Don't you know that either? Goddamn it," he exploded, "what goes on? The Cupid. This Cavalli calls me yesterday and claims he's pulling out. He claims it's over to you." He explained tersely about Cavalli's latest telephone call.

"Ah yes, the Cupid," d'Espinal murmured. "I see." The devil of it was that one did not see, except that this must be some curious ploy of Raven's. He watched Graziella coming with a tray and three more cups, but not the child.

Emilia's face was expressionless, but Judith Teestock remarked, "I don't wonder you have stomach ulcers, Mr. Polliano." It was difficult to tell whether she was critical or sympathetic. "Milk or lemon?" she asked, and Ricci whispered something; Alberto laughed suddenly.

"You'll take tea and like it," Polliano snarled at them once more and then demanded, "God's sake, why's everybody so cagey about this thing?"

"I do not know," d'Espinal told him. "Nor do I know Mr. Cavalli. I have heard of the Cupid, yes, but I have never seen it."

"He's stalling," Ricci complained. "You want we should go over this place, Polly?"

"Indeed you will not." Mrs. Teestock was magnificently outraged, and d'Espinal got up slowly; he did not much care for this kind of crudity, but Emilia was watching him.

"I have never seen the Cupid," he repeated. "I am not interested in the Cupid. Nor in you gentlemen. I suggest you leave; the ladies do not like your company." Melodramatic again, he told himself irritably.

Polliano's voice was so soft suddenly that it startled them. "Riding over here, Ricci, I said to take it easy. Don't you get the message? Pardon me, ma'am," he apologized to Mrs. Teestock, "but we get the feeling we've been taken for a monkey and it annoys us."

"As well it might," d'Espinal conceded. He brooded for a moment and said, "Like you, I also am annoyed. I do not understand this but I suspect an unpardonable impertinence, and one feels we should correct it severely. We are, as it were, on the same side, Mr. Polliano. Indeed, if you were to tell us a little more, in particular how you heard of the Cupid and your own interest, we might try to help you."

For one wild moment Emilia wanted to warn Polliano, tell him that whatever he might be he was no match for that big, devious, permanently fascinating rogue, but she said nothing, and he asked, "Why not?" He added surprisingly, "You ever been in this place, the Medici Chapel, in Florence? You seen the statues?" D'Espinal nodded, and Polliano went on, "They're quite something. Well, I have an idea a while back. Maybe it was screwy but it looked like a good idea when I first got it, it looked like a nice thing to do. So I call my mouthpiece." He glanced at Mrs. Teestock again. "Lawyer, ma'am. I tell him, 'Tullio, I want a statue or some such by this Michelangelo—not too big, but good. Find me some guy who knows how.' So in a week or so Tullio comes back and says the guy I want is named Sabbioni. You know that Sabbioni?"

"I have heard of him," d'Espinal admitted.

"Seems you can't meet this guy, he's so goddamned old, so I call him, and he says he don't know of nothing for the present, there's not a lot of them around, but he'll ask people. But it'll take time and cost big money. And I say that's okay by me."

"How long ago was this?"

"Way back. Eight months or more. Then he calls me two, three times, claims he's still looking, and maybe he does hear of something. And about a month back he says he has for sure, and he don't want to deal with it, he's too old, but if I come to Venice and have a piece put in the *Gazzettino*—'Mr. Polliano and party have arrived'—and the hotel, somebody will be in touch. This I do and sure enough I get a package by mail. A wad of papers and photographs. Say," he asked peevishly, "is that a regular way of doing business?"

"One can imagine occasions when it might be," d'Espinal said guardedly. "Pray continue, Mr. Polliano." He listened in his habitual pose—eyes half closed and chin sunk on his chest—until Polliano finished, and then said, "So to summarize. In telephone negotiations only, the price was brought up to one million. But on Monday Cavalli actually called on you personally and offered the Cupid for one half of that against a quick settlement through the Bank of America and Italy. Yet on Tuesday he telephoned once more to say I had taken over the matter. Is that correct?"

Polliano nodded. "So for God's sake, what goes on?"

D'Espinal looked like a Roman emperor contemplating something extremely unpleasant to do with the arena. "One would say some disagreement among the vendors. And quite considerable intrigue and incompetence."

"Sure. But where do you fit in?"

"At this present I do not. When I do, if I do, I will apprise you of the fact."

Polliano blinked at him. "You mean you ain't talking?"

"There is nothing to talk about."

"Seems we don't get no place." Polliano pushed himself up slowly. "See here, Mr. d'Espinal, I don't place you. But you might be on the level, so on the level I'll talk. There was a time, only three, four days back, when I get to thinking the hell with it, I don't want this Cupid so bad after all, it ain't worth the guts ache. Pardon, ma'am," he added automatically. "I get near enough to saying we'll throw the hand in and pull out for Rome. But not any more, Mr. d'Espinal. Nobody ever plays Iccy P. for a sucker and wins. I mean to have that goddamned baby now if it's the last thing I ever get on this earth."

"And presumably at your own price?" d'Espinal asked.

"Just say I mean to have it. Come on, boys. Let's go."

"Hold it, Polly," Alberto said. "What about that kid?"

"What about her?" Polliano asked. "Be your age, 'Berto. I said to come on."

They watched them going across the grass, the motor coughing to life in the quietness, the boat surging away and becoming unsubstantial again in the haze, vanishing as if it had never been here, and Mrs. Teestock breathed, "Well . . ."

"Why is it," d'Espinal inquired, "that when one seeks the last word it never comes readily to the lips?"

"I've a feeling that the last word could easily be unpleasant," Emilia said. "What are you going to do?"

The surprisingly wolfish look which d'Espinal sometimes assumed appeared momentarily on his face. "I really don't feel we can allow Colonel Raven and his Signor Cavalli to have it all their own way. At least, my dear, we can now see the whole pattern. I find it singularly unattractive but, as I have said before, not unamusing."

"And that child? She was badly frightened. Harry, is it possible that somehow she's involved?"

"A stone child or a real one, and which is worth the most?" He looked at Emilia sadly. "I think I thought of that one before too. Let us go and look for little Angela, my dear."

"And see if you can talk some sense into her," Mrs. Teestock suggested.

By half past eight Bruno Cavalli was more surprised

than angry. He had thought that Angela would certainly come back for five thousand lire and another meal. But it did not matter much now, and he had far more agreeable things to think about: the nine o'clock Trans-Europa for Milan, a fast journey and a pleasant night with an engaging and agreeable young lady, a satisfactorily profitable little business meeting before lunch tomorrow. It was good also for Raven to realize that one had other affairs on hand. A pity that one ever had to come back to this moldering heap of old stone falling into its own canals, but it need only be for a few more days, and not for anything could he miss that final ceremony in the Bank of America and Italy. He must be on hand to produce the Cupid when Mr. Harcourt d'Espinal arranged the deal for them. In the meantime it would sleep quietly and safely where it was.

He left for Santa Lucia Station just five minutes before Ricci and Alberto arrived, moving up silently out of the deserted *campo;* Polly reckoned they could not snatch the kid off San Giorgio because that Limey knew who they were, but at least they could shake this little crook out. Ricci cursed briefly, finding the apartment in darkness and the door locked, but with a confidence born of false security Cavalli had left a slip of paper pinned there. In the small flame of Ricci's cigarette lighter it read obligingly: "Signora Tasso, I return Friday evening. Leave my laundry here." Alberto muttered, "Kinda simple, ain't he?"

At about that time on San Giorgio—while Angela lay awake and resentful of being sent to bed so early, still slightly afraid those men might come back for her yet, even though Signor d'Espinal said they would not dare, feeling that she herself had talked too much while Signorina Emilia made that wonderful picture of her—Mrs. Teestock, Emilia and d'Espinal were sitting with their coffee under the vines. It was quite dark now, the lights of Murano and Venice glittering distantly across the lagoon: a faintly luminous sheet of silk which changed suddenly into ruffled velvet as an uneasy little breeze swept across. Mrs. Teestock said, "There'll be rain soon. Tomorrow perhaps." She was faintly affronted by Emilia and Harcourt being apparently so successful with the child, and asked again, "But did she not give you any hint of where she comes from?"

"We didn't ask. We only encouraged her to talk." Emilia turned to glance across at d'Espinal and he thought she looked even more uncommonly handsome than usual tonight, in this soft light against the dusky background of the garden. But she seemed worried, as he was himself. She asked, "Do you think they really did try to run her down?"

"I don't know," he admitted. "It seems so purposeless. And why give her five thousand lire afterwards?"

"What was it your friend in Trastevere said? 'A sick old tiger who might go hunting again.' And she admits she's been following Cavalli for days."

There was a touch of asperity in Mrs. Teestock's voice. "She really does seem to have told you a great deal."

"Darling," Emilia explained, "it was only doing the portrait. That broke her reserve."

"It enchanted her," d'Espinal corrected. "And so it should have done." He brooded over the brandy glass cupped between his palms, reached forward and set it down on the table with a sharp little click. "There's much more she's not telling us. Why did Cavalli want her to fetch this Mario on Monday night? Why did Cavalli 'vanish' on the San Niccolò road? And if those fellows did try to run her down, why was it in the same place? What was she doing there herself?"

Mrs. Teestock was not so easily mollified. "It could be pure fantasy. Even deliberate lying to explain all that money. Which Mrs. Pietro is quite convinced she's stolen."

Emilia shook her head. "I don't think so. There's something there she's just simply obstinate about. I think she's nursing some final secret of her own, something which fascinates and rather frightens her at the same time."

"You may well be right," d'Espinal agreed. "I am learning a great respect for your understanding, my dear. She might tell us herself in time. We might see a little more clearly ourselves after I have talked very plainly to this precious pair, Raven and Cavalli, to-morrow. But if, as I begin to suspect, they are using a child . . ." There was a look on his face which Emilia did not like; it was possible even to be a little afraid of Harcourt sometimes. He said, "We should be wise to assume that Angela Caterina is in some danger. We must find out why. And she must stay here for a few days."

"But that's impossible," Mrs. Teestock protested. "It's illegal. We can't keep her prisoner."

"Dear lady," he told her, "I fear the nice point of legality was left behind some little time ago, if it ever existed. Angela Caterina must not be allowed to leave San Giorgio until we have this whole affair cleared up."

Chapter Eight

Unfortunately they did not tell Mrs. Pietro of the necessity to keep the child on the island, and both she and Angela had their own intentions. Mrs. Pietro proceeded with her plans not from any malice but simply because one had to protect the padrona, who, although a great lady, was in many ways very innocent and was imposed upon more often than she realized. And as for Signor d'Espinal, even Pietro—who considered the sun shone out of his face, and the sooner he and Signorina Pentecost made a match of it the better—agreed that he could be almost as easily taken in too. It was all quite simple. She and Pietro always went to the Rialto markets on Friday mornings, and it was perfectly clear that the child was itching to get back to Venice and her thieving tricks as fast as she could. So if she came across just for the boat ride and then chose to walk off into the crowds, nobody could be blamed.

That suited Angela perfectly too; she did not like Mrs. Pietro much either. Skimming across the shining, early-morning lagoon, clutching her hat and the precious portrait, she thought contentedly that there was a lot to tell Signor Cavalli now: she knew nearly everything about Isola San Giorgio Piccolo, and he would be particularly interested in this picture. She was really rather clever, she thought complacently, and the new sandals were almost a certainty. After that, one would work out what to do next, but clearly just knowing where the stone baby was must be worth a lot of money too, and she would probably tell Signor d'Espinal and Signorina Emilia in the end. They at least had been very understanding.

When they stopped at the Rialto and went ashore into the chatter and bustle of the markets, she said politely, "Thank you for your kindness, signore, signora. And will you please say to Signor d'Espinal that if he comes to Venice tomorrow I might have something to inform him."

Facing Colonel Raven across the desk in his study, the green water ripples still dancing and flickering on the ceiling, d'Espinal was both angry and far more worried than he would have cared to admit—as much by Angela's extraordinary message as by the fact of her disappearance. Pietro and Emilia were already searching for her, and Pietro would tell his friends to look out too, but the child might have a hundred hiding places. One could only guess what mischief she was about. He would join them himself as soon as possible, when he had settled with this silly fellow here. He said, "I consider it was damned impudence and a damned mischievous blunder."

Raven seemed to be amused. "Typical of Cavalli."

"Are you telling me," d'Espinal demanded, "that only Cavalli planned that farce yesterday?"

"I'm telling you the man can't resist intrigue."

"And I suggest that you yourself arranged it, no doubt with Cavalli, to drag me into this mess of incompetence. To become what I believe is called the front man, in case of danger. It does not please me, Colonel Raven."

"No?" The colonel smiled suddenly, a surprising and deceitful flash of charm. "Very well, then. Let's call it a mistake. But at least it's brought you here today. And I'm hoping you'll see your own best interests."

D'Espinal asked softly, "What exactly do you mean by that?"

"Need we go into it now? Why don't we work together, Mr. d'Espinal? My only concern is to sell that Cupid. As quickly as possible, and for the highest possible price. It should be quite simple."

"You are simple yourself, sir. Have you ever stopped to ask why Cavalli is so nervous?"

"He says so plainly enough. He's afraid that Polliano might make off with the Cupid and leave him with nothing but a broken head—or worse."

"I can suggest half a dozen methods of circumventing any such stratagem without even stopping to think. So, I am sure, can Signor Cavalli." D'Espinal smiled unpleasantly. "No, sir. Your Cavalli is afraid of what Mr. Polliano and his bullies might do if he is persuaded to buy something as a Michelangelo and then later discovers it to be a worthless forgery. He is quite right. They are Sicilians, I understand, and Sicilians do not take lightly to such frolics."

Raven asked, "Are you suggesting . . . ?"

"I am telling you, sir, in so many words. The Cupid is a forgery—worth about a thousand dollars. Created by a master, in his own way, but not a Michelangelo.

And your Bruno Cavalli knows it. In his place I should be having sleepless nights myself."

The colonel stared at him for a long ten seconds, while it was so quiet that one could hear his elegant little silver traveling clock ticking, and then exploded, "That's damnation nonsense! Sabbioni vouched for it himself. You've seen all the papers."

"Sabbioni," d'Espinal said indulgently, "is a most ingenious old rascal. Colonel Raven," he asked, "you are working on a new biography of Benito Mussolini, with particular reference to his last days and the mystery of the Dongo treasure?"

"That's no secret."

"Why should it be? Therefore you would know that Niccolò Sabbioni was an acquaintance of Mussolini's in those early days before the war? And you approached him?"

"Obviously. He could give me first-hand information. I wrote to him originally, about a year ago. Then I met him, in some bar on the Via Veneto—Rosati's. After that I called at the apartment, when he loaned me a bundle of old diaries and letters."

"Beautiful," d'Espinal murmured. "And did you go into that big room with windows overlooking the Pinciana Gate?"

"No. The old man was unwell. I was taken into his bedroom."

"A pity. Had you entered the other you would have seen your little Cupid already reclining there." Raven sat watching d'Espinal bleakly, and d'Espinal asked, "May I continue? To your researches at Garzeno, in the early spring this year. I suggest that some person or persons then approached you with the information that he or they knew where at least one forgotten item of the Dongo treasure was lying. In short, on the farm of Domenico Galli. Am I correct?"

"More or less."

"And you found the Cupid with Galli's assistance?"

"It was half buried in dung."

"A pleasantly bucolic touch. And then of course you could be expected to purchase it from Galli and send it to the one great authority you knew for appraisal—Niccolò Sabbioni again. I imagine that your delight and surprise, on being advised that you had actually unearthed the lost Cupid of Michelangelo, must have been a joy to behold. How much did the old rogue tell you it was worth?"

"Upwards of a million dollars."

D'Espinal sighed. "Let us not indulge in vain speculation. I would say that Sabbioni then offered to undertake further research on your behalf. In the course of which it was discovered that so far from being part of Mussolini's treasure the Cupid had in fact been lying in the village unrecognized since 1631, as witness the good Father Rossi's letter of 1720. And by some Divine coincidence your interest in one treasure had led you straight to another. As pretty a little swindle as I've ever known concocted."

"You haven't a shred of evidence anywhere."

D'Espinal looked reproachful. "I never make any statement without evidence. I know that Polliano requested Sabbioni to look for a work by Michelangelo some two months or more before you found the Cupid. The thing was planted there for you to discover, my dear fellow. In effect Sabbioni was selling it himself, but only at a distance safely removed and through the intermediary of two more persons: yourself and this somewhat ridiculous Cavalli. By so doing Sabbioni would of course lose two thirds of the figure ultimately realized, but still receive a very handsome price for a comparatively worthless object. Also, I fancy the notion amused him. It amuses me."

"You can't prove anything. Sabbioni's documents are as good as your word."

"There was a flaw in the original marble which Alceo Dossena worked. That I have from Niccolò Sabbioni himself. It can still be seen in your Sleeping Cupid."

"And who was Alceo Dossena?" Raven asked bleakly.

"The one man without whom the whole frolic would have been impossible. Probably the only artist-craftsman in history who could successfully imitate Michelangelo." Time was pressing, and they really must find that child quickly, but he could at least spare another few minutes to instruct this innocent and ignorant colonel. He started remorselessly, "Alceo Dossena, still an enigma . . ."

Raven listened without interrupting, thinking coldly that the man was merely a fat poseur who had his own surprise to come in a few minutes, and d'Espinal worked up to his final peroration. "So, set up by this Alfredo Fasoli in the small studio by the Tiber in 1918, Dossena's underground fame grew among the dealers. Over the next ten years he created a succession of works—an Athene, a Tomb of the Savelli, a Madonna and Child and many more—some of which are still unknown, and all in different styles. His Athene has been compared favorably with the greatest of Classical art; the Tomb of the Savelli was hailed as a Renaissance masterpiece and finally sold for six million lire— a lot of money in those days. Incidentally, it was accompanied by a receipt to the Savelli family signed by Mino da Fiesole himself. You will notice the parallel with your own charming letter by the dear old priest Father Rossi of 1720, who describes 'a small pagan statue' and says it has been in the village since his grandfather's time."

"Are you claiming that letter is a forgery too?"

"My dear sir, of course it's a forgery, arranged by Cavalli. Let us return to Alceo Dossena. The poor fellow was periodically addicted to women and wine, always the flowery path to poverty. Moreover, by now he had got wind of the very large figures which were being paid for his work, and in 1928 he went to the dealer who had recently sold his Madonna and Child by Pisano for three million lire and asked for an advance on his next work. It was refused—somewhat brutally. And, in a word, he blew the gaff, and some of the greatest names were threatened, some of the brightest reputations began to look a little tarnished."

"Mr. d'Espinal," Raven interrupted, "I don't care a damn who made that Cupid, I am going to sell it. Or rather, you are going to sell it for me."

D'Espinal opened his eyes for a long, hard look and murmured, "No doubt in your profession you are used to giving orders. In mine I am not accustomed to taking them."

"No?" the colonel asked expressionlessly. "I'd hoped we might arrange this more pleasantly. I did mention your own best interests."

"You did indeed." D'Espinal was just as expressionless.

"I hope we don't have to talk about it," Raven said. "Or Miss Emilia Pentecost."

"I hope not." D'Espinal brooded over that for a few seconds and then got up slowly. "I hope not, for your sake." He asked, "What do you propose?"

"Merely that you should get Polliano up to a million dollars, and then fix a date when we can meet and settle the whole thing. Cavalli suggests at the Bank of America and Italy."

"It all sounds exquisitely simple. But I must talk to Cavalli first. Where can I find him?"

"I don't see why you need. But if you must, he has an apartment on the Campo Sant' Anna. He's in Milan on some business of his own today. He'll be back in Venice this evening."

"And the Cupid itself? I must examine that."

"Cavalli will produce it when necessary." Raven hesitated. "He's hidden the thing."

"He's what?" D'Espinal looked at the colonel incredulously. "Hidden it? In Heaven's name why? And where?"

"Why? Because that's the way his mind works. And if I knew where I should go and get it myself."

"This becomes a farce." In fact it was a damned nuisance. It destroyed one small stratagem he was already considering, and it began to look as if these incompetents were really rather more clever than he had first supposed. He pondered over that unpleasantly and then said, "Very well. Then I must have the original Sabbioni documents."

Raven turned bleak again. "No, Mr. d'Espinal. I keep those."

"Pray let us be sensible," d'Espinal begged. "No man can be expected to talk in terms of a million on the strength of a nonappearing statue and a bundle of photostats. I must have those documents. Or," he added piously, "I must warn Polliano that you personally are proposing to perpetrate a singularly audacious swindle on him."

The colonel thought about that too, at last opened the desk drawer and took out a bulky envelope, pushing it across. "Be very careful with them," he advised. "And don't be too long about the arrangement, Mr. d'Espinal. In your own interest."

"I shall not be too long," d'Espinal promised. "But as to whose interest is perhaps a different matter."

By eleven o'clock Angela knew they were looking for her. She had already been to the Campo Sant' Anna, read Cavalli's obliging note and, still clutching her portrait, worked over towards the markets for something to eat. And Pietro was there, looking round the stalls. She only escaped by slipping into the crowd, and then when she tried to get back over the Rialto Bridge he was waiting there again, watching the only exit to the Saint Mark's side of the canal. In succession after that she just as narrowly evaded a boatman calling, "Eh! Stop there, you," Emilia on the Accademia, a gondolier who tried to hold her, and Ricci and Alberto. It was like some kind of sunlit nightmare in harsh colors and black shadows, as if every *calle* she turned into were waiting for her, everybody who passed were going to say, "Wait a minute, little girl."

D'Espinal, Emilia and Pietro had arranged to meet at the Campanile by twelve thirty—the simplest thing they could do, and it gave each of them a chance of quartering a different area in the time. D'Espinal was there when Emilia arrived, and he asked quickly, "Well? Have you seen her?"

"On the Accademia," Emilia said. "But she saw me too, coming down the steps from the bridge. That child can disappear like a cat. And, Harry, the others are here. Polliano's men. They were crossing the square."

D'Espinal muttered something under his breath. "Are they looking for her, do you think?"

"They didn't appear to be. I don't see how they can know she's in Venice yet. But with that hat . . ."

"I take your point." He looked across the vast square with its drifting, murmuring crowds. "Like trying to find a pebble on the beach. It's a confounded tangle now, Emilia. It seems this ineffectual idiot Cavalli has hidden the Cupid. I more than suspect the child knows where. And if those ugly brutes realize that—" He stopped and finished, "Here's Pietro."

Pietro at least was enjoying himself; this was better than working drowsily on San Giorgio. He announced cheerfully, "That's a slippery little devil. I nearly got her, heading for the Rialto Bridge, but she was too fast for me."

"The Rialto Bridge, the Accademia Bridge," d'Espinal said. "She's trying to cross over to this side. What for, I wonder? To reach Cavalli? Don't forget she took your portrait with her, Emilia. But he doesn't get back here until tonight, and she probably knows that." He watched two of the municipal guards parading solemnly under the arcade. "I must tell you, my dear. I think we should have the police looking for her."

"And tell them what?" Emilia asked sharply. "No, Harry. She'd never forgive us. What's the other place she's so fond of? The Exposition Gardens. Why don't we look there?"

"We can try perhaps, and then work back to this Campo Sant' Anna, where it appears Cavalli lives. But I cannot disguise my forebodings." He turned again to Pietro. "Pietro, old friend, there's one more thing, if you'll bear with us. I want you to look for a person named Mario. He is a boatman and he works between the markets and the hotels in the early mornings. Spend what you like, fill him up with wine if you must, but find out what Signor Bruno Cavalli wanted him for, and presumably his boat, late on Monday night. We'll meet back here at four o'clock."

With frightened obstinacy, surveying every narrow passage before she turned into it, Angela set out to plod northwards all the way to the Scalzi Bridge, the last on the Grand Canal, to circle back again to the one safe place she knew: her secret corner on the roof of the empty palace in the Campo Sant' Anna. It was now breathlessly hot, and all over Venice people were starting to look up at the sky for that coppery thickening which always presaged one of their violent autumnal storms. So hot that, with the heat bearing down like a suffocating blanket from the tall, peeling walls leaning over them, Ricci and Alberto at last gave up the chase blasphemously in a blind, ancient maze of *calli* and silent waterways, while Pietro, sweating and cursing softly, worked round the half-deserted and almost totally somnolent markets looking for Mario, and Emilia and d'Espinal started slowly back from the gardens at the other end of the city to move in on Saint Mark's Square and the Campanile once more. By the time they reached it Angela was curled up like a kitten in her corner of the rooftop, still clutching the rather crumpled portrait, feeling drowsily that she had really been very clever again.

When Emilia and d'Espinal reached the Campanile, Pietro was sitting on the steps fanning himself with the jaunty yachting cap he affected. He announced, "There's going to be a wicked storm," and then, "Well, I found that character for you, Signor d'Espinal. The devil of a hunt, but I found him at last sleeping in his boat. Couldn't fill the scoundrel up with wine though, couldn't get any more in."

"What did he say?" Emilia asked quickly.

"Nothing, or very little. Only that the girl will get her head knocked in before she's done. I dangled a thousand-lire note under his nose and he laughed at me. So I told him I'd heard he had a brutal trip all in the dark on Monday night, and he closed up like an oyster. Just drunk enough to be cunning. Except to grunt some rubbish about be damned to haunted graveyards, and whatever was going on he wanted no part of it."

"Haunted graveyards?" d'Espinal repeated. His hot, flushed face took on a look of faintly petulant perplexity. "My dear fellow, what on earth does that mean?"

Pietro scratched his head doubtfully. "Come to think of it, I suppose they're all haunted more or less. Can't say that graveyards interest me much. Not yet anyhow. I could ask Mama Pietro when we get back. She's full of tales like that."

"Does it matter?" Emilia asked impatiently. "Are we trying to find the Cupid or Angela Caterina?"

"The child, of course. But I feel certain now that she knows where it is. If we find one we might well find the other."

"If you ask me," Pietro said, "nobody who doesn't have to be is about in this heat. Only the tourists. That child's sleeping quietly somewhere and she won't come out again until it cools off. She's a cunning little devil."

"Eminently sensible, as ever, Pietro," d'Espinal agreed. "Very well, then, we'll return to San Giorgio Piccolo and you shall ask Mrs. Pietro about haunted graveyards. It's possible too that Angela might try to get in touch with Cavalli. So I shall come back tonight to see him instead of tomorrow."

Angela was sitting with her hands clasped round her knees watching night creep in over the rooftops, the lagoon deepening to purple between a fairy-tale jumble of red tiles, gray and dull-gold steeples and domes, the tracery of pinnacles and statues washed over by a shimmering haze. The noise of the city came up remotely: hammering in a boatyard, a gondolier singing on the Canal of the Apostles down at the front of the palace. She had counted seven strokes from all the clocks a long time ago; the ghosts would soon be starting to stir and wander in the old, deserted rooms

below, but with so many people looking for her it
was better to wait until it was quite dark before ven-
turing out.

She waited deliberately for the bells to chime out
again, eight o'clock this time, before creeping down
the broken stairs, feeling her way, listening for every
sound above her own breathing and at last crouching
by the boarded window, peering out on the campo.
Enclosed by the tall old buildings it was like a quiet
pool of heat, still deserted, the one dim lamp burning
under the archway, another gleaming faintly on the
water. But Signor Cavalli's window and door were lit
too, so he was home at last. She watched while a barge
passed slowly along the canal, and then ran across fast,
suddenly and breathlessly longing for light and
company.

Up on the balcony the door was open, but no sign
of Signor Cavalli. There was nobody in the kitchen,
and she stood there looking at a broken glass glittering
on the tiled floor, the table pushed askew, one of the
stools lying on its side and the other door into the little
passage open. At first she was puzzled rather than
frightened, and she edged in silently, listening, creeping as far as the other door and into the passage itself.
Three more doors, all of them open, lights on everywhere, someone moving and whispering, cursing softly,
in the room on the left. Feeling her own heart thumping as if it did not belong to her, she edged in a few
more paces, and even as she reached the doorway one
voice, so close and harsh that she choked on a scream,
said, "Goddamn you, 'Berto, I said to take it easy."

It was like seeing a picture. Signor Cavalli lying on
his back with arms and legs trailing, crumpled over a

shattered chair, his head hanging and mouth and eyes open, staring right at her and horribly upside down, the big wooden box with a litter of cotton packing tossed out on the carpet. The two gray men were there, the small spiteful one bending over Signor Cavalli, whispering, "You goddamned fool," clutching his jacket front with both hands as if trying to shake him to life again, and the other with his back to Angela, standing slackly and swearing, "Hell, Ricci, the bastard just folded, I didn't hit him all that—" Then Angela caught her breath, a harsh sound in her throat, and Ricci's head jerked up, staring at her like a vicious dog. For one long second she was too frozen to move. She heard him hiss, "Jeez, the kid," and then with her first scream she fled.

It was the ruinous old sandals again. Back into the kitchen and nearly at the door, with all of that comforting darkness out there to hide in, when one of them twisted under her. Within reach of the balcony she fell sprawling, heard herself cry out, although it was little more than a breathless wail, and then Alberto was on her. Half dazed, she was dragged up, flung back against the table and held there. A door slammed while she opened her lips for another scream, but the big, soft hand clamped over her mouth and nose. She could feel tears running down her cheeks, and there was a pounding noise in her ears, but through it she just caught someone saying, "Hold it, 'Berto," and then snarling, "Goddamn it, I said to hold it."

Somehow then she was free, crouching against the table and feeling her ankle painful where the broken sandal had twisted, but still free to take deep, sobbing

breaths. Both were watching her and quite still and
quiet suddenly until Ricci spoke again, this time in a
soft, kind voice. He said, "You got the wrong idea,
kid. Here," hooking the stool upright. "Sit down. Get
your breath. You got the wrong idea. Your friend took
a sort of fit. We was trying to help him. Come on now,
sit down," he encouraged her. "We don't like to see a
kid so scared." There was nothing else she could do,
and edging across to the stool she sat down, automatically bringing up her foot to tie on the loose sandal, looking at Alberto warily and glancing sideways at
her hat lying near the door. Ricci himself picked it
up and gave it to her, saying, "That's a real pretty
hat."

"Ricci," Alberto muttered. Angela saw him glance
at her.

"Sure," Ricci agreed softly, "but not here." He
smiled, and that terrified Angela afresh. "We could go
find a doctor for poor Mr. Cavalli. But maybe the little
girl tells us something first. Like what she's doing
around here."

She peered at him tearfully. "Signor Cavalli said
to come. He sometimes gave me something to eat.
What happened to him?"

"Like I told you. He took a kind of fit."

She knew that was a lie. There was an old man at
Chioggia who was always having fits and he never
looked anything like that. They had killed Signor
Cavalli because they wanted the stone baby, and quite
clearly they would kill her too unless she could think
of something—perhaps tell them she would not go to
the police. And be careful not to get frightened again
because being frightened made you do foolish things;

Signorina Emilia had said that yesterday while drawing her portrait. She wondered vaguely where the picture was; she must have dropped it somewhere, she thought, but it did not matter much now. Nothing mattered. Only getting out of here into the friendly darkness. She whispered, "I shall not tell the police. I promise."

Alberto moved behind her again, but Ricci said, "Now there's a thing. Why should you go to the cops anyway?"

"Because . . ." She realized her mistake too late. "I don't know. I mean, I don't like the police either. They cause trouble."

"What're we waiting for?" Alberto asked.

Angela knew that was for her. She tried to twist round to look at Alberto, but Ricci was still watching her, and she whispered, "Please. I can tell you all about Signor Cavalli. I can tell you where he took the stone baby. I know where it is."

Ricci said, "Well, that's fine. Ain't that fine, 'Berto? She's a real clever kid. And we can't leave her here all alone with poor Mr. Cavalli. People might get to asking why we were so thoughtless. So why don't she tell us where this baby is? Then maybe we could find some nice place and give the kid her supper. D'you get the message, 'Berto?"

"Sure," Alberto agreed. "There's a plenty of nice places. So where is that baby, kid? And how come you know?"

"I was watching him, from the old palace. He took it in a boat." She stopped suddenly. It would have been much better to have told them he had hidden it in the old palace itself, then she might get them inside and somehow escape in the absolute darkness there. One could trick them quite easily, and then there would still be five thousand lire when she told Signor d'Espinal where the baby was. She tried again. "He took it into the old palace at the end of the *campo* here."

Ricci shook his head slowly. He reached out and slapped her face. "That's what comes to kids who don't tell the truth. He took it in a boat, like you said first. So where did he take it?"

"To the Lido," she wept. "There is an old grave-yard there. I know because I found it myself. That day you tried to—" She caught her breath and stopped again.

"That day we tried to do what?" Ricci asked. "You get some funny ideas, kid." He nodded to Alberto. "Okay, 'Berto, we got to go back to the Lido too, so why don't we have her along and find this baby?" It could be she was lying, he thought, but the sooner they were out of this place the better. There was nothing to tie them up with Cavalli—clean up the door handles and they were quit of it—but the cops had already seen them with this little bastard. Best have no connections and nobody would worry much about a beggar brat found in a canal. He said, "Okay. Let's go." Opening the door, he looked out over the balcony and said, "Take her down. And wait."

Angela went without resistance, hoping that Alberto could not hear her heart thumping. But going down the narrow stone steps she managed to work her toes out of one sandal after the other, and when they came out onto the *campo* she stood quite slackly, supremely confident once more that Sant' Anna would help her again. She asked, "When we've found the stone baby where will you take me to have supper? I know a very nice place on the Lido. A friend of mine."

Alberto laughed quietly. "Sure, kid. Anywhere. A supper like you never had before." He breathed, "What's keeping you, Ricci?" but the grip on her shoulder loosened slightly.

She said innocently, "That will be very good, I am nearly always hungry," and glanced back at the archway opposite, with its one dim lamp barely twenty meters away, and at the same time Ricci appeared on the balcony. He seemed to be polishing at the door handle. Then Angela whispered, "I think we should be careful, signore. There are two *carabinieri*, at the end of the *calle* there."

Alberto was looking up, watching Ricci, but he jerked his head round at once and the fingers at her shoulder slackened still more. She moved as fast as a small, savage animal again. Twisting her own head, she bit at his wrist and at the same time lashed up with her right hand to claw at his face. He grunted and cursed, but somehow she wrenched herself free, racing barefoot for the *calle* and the darkness beyond.

Chapter Nine

It was a series of simple human failings which made them late. Mrs. Pietro still offended by the fuss over that girl this morning. Judith Teestock equally offended by her ingratitude, convinced she could more than take care of herself, and insisting that they must not go off again before dinner and upset Mrs. Pietro even more. Pietro knowing better than to ask silly questions about haunted graveyards with Mama Pietro in her present mood. D'Espinal feeling unhappily that it was he who had brought this element of discord into the normal serenity of San Giorgio Piccolo, persuading himself too that no harm could come to the child tonight. By the time Graziella brought in the coffee he was about to suggest that they should leave it all until tomorrow, even ask Emilia to play the piano for them, when she herself threw down her napkin and said, "No, Judith, I'm sorry. We must find her quickly. Don't ask me why, but I can feel it."

They lost still more time through the network of waterways in the Sant' Anna area, and it was well after nine when Pietro at last turned cautiously into the quiet canal. There was only one lighted window on the campo, and leaving Pietro in the boat they hurried across, stopping only for a second to look up at the balcony before turning to the steps. Emilia found the sandals, stumbling over the first one, feeling what it was in the darkness and groping for the other, and then, in the better light on the balcony itself, said, "Angela's." D'Espinal nodded, ringing the doorbell, knocking and rattling the door. Emilia said urgently, "Open it."

Inside they stood looking at the table pushed aside, a stool lying on the floor and glittering fragments of broken glass, and listening, as d'Espinal said afterwards, to altogether too much silence. He called, "Signor Cavalli!" and it sounded to both of them like shattering something tangible. Emilia again first saw the portrait—a small crumbled roll lying under a side table in the hall—and while she was opening it out, starting to say something herself, she heard d'Espinal whisper, "Dear God." He was standing at the other doorway and she moved over to him, just three paces, catching her own breath sharply, staring past him at the bruised, inverted face and bluish lips, a thin line of blood trickling perversely from one corner of the open mouth to the eye, the head almost hanging into a packing case and a mess of cotton waste.

Back in the kitchen Emilia asked, "Well?"

D'Espinal closed the outer door carefully. "It looks as if he died of heart failure. Or terror. He was beaten about."

She dropped the sandals and portrait onto the table. "I don't mean that. I mean the girl."

"I don't know," he said. "But there's one thing certain. We can't leave the poor devil lying like that. It's indecent."

"The police?"

"We must. But whatever we do might be wrong. It was Polliano's people almost certainly." He stopped, flattening out the portrait and studying it. "It's a delightful drawing, my dear, and indefinably Renaissance. She came to show it Cavalli, of course. But did she come afterwards, or while those ugly morons were still here?"

"If she did . . ."

"I don't know," he told her again and then asked, "You found the sandals close together. Wouldn't you think that if those animals had carried or dragged her one might have fallen here, the other some distance away? Is it possible she shook them off herself? To run the better?"

"I hope so. What are you going to tell the police?"

"No more than I need. About those vicious brutes. And I must describe the child. We daren't risk otherwise. They should be searching within minutes."

He turned back into the hallway. Emilia heard him dialing and moved out restlessly onto the balcony herself. By leaning over she could see Pietro waiting in the boat, his white cap and the glow of a cigarette. It was difficult to believe that they had not been here for much more than five minutes; difficult in this silent old square to believe also that barely more than a hundred yards away there were streets blazing with lights and shops, thronged with strolling, chattering crowds. Through the open doorway she heard d'Espinal raise his voice slightly. "No, signore, I shall not wait for you. I propose to start looking for this child myself, and at once. I repeat, I am Harcourt d'Espinal, resident on Isola San Giorgio Piccolo, a guest of Mrs. Judith

Teestock. Yes, of course you've heard of Mrs. Teestock. And if you require further assurance I'm sure Mrs. Messina-Silvestro will be happy to supply it."

He came out with the faintly wolfish expression on his face. "One should never hesitate to drop a good name. Now we must find this naughty child before the police. We'll have Pietro take us back to the Rialto, leave the boat there and all three scour every street back to Saint Mark's and the waterfront. I've a feeling she'll run for people and lights. And somehow I must find time to telephone old Paolo and Annunzietta. They might know where or what this haunted graveyard is. I'm certain that's the heart of the whole business." Taking the sandals and the portrait, they ran down the steps and out to the *campo*, and he breathed, "I believe it's getting hotter. I always said there was a hint of hell in anything old Sabbioni touches."

"That's ridiculous," Emilia said. "It's the storm. It's going to break soon—anytime now."

Angela crouched under a bridge, peering back along the water. There was nobody to be seen and no sound of footsteps. This was after a great many corners, crossing several canals by jumping from one moored barge to another, and by now she must have lost Alberto and Ricci. They were really rather stupid, she considered. Her shirt was torn and her shoulder sore, but there was a good, spiteful satisfaction in remembering the last glimpse of Alberto, blundering clumsily after her with one hand to his face while she streaked for the archway and Ricci clattered down the steps. After that if they caught her again they would certainly kill her, so it was time to move on to where there were more people. This place was too quiet; if a rat moved here it made a noise. Blind old buildings leaning against the sky, a dark canal moving sluggishly in the light of one bracket lamp, a black string of tied-up boats. Somewhere not far off a police siren wailed, a launch shot past the far end of the cutting with its searchlight flickering momentarily over the crumbling old arches, and she slipped off again silently.

They were barely two blocks away in a small, empty bar, Ricci expressionless with rage, Alberto dabbing at his face and eye, the barman watching them warily while they talked in whispers. Alberto grunted, "She's wicked, that kid. She might've blinded me. Jeez, I get her now I break her clean in half. So if we don't get her maybe she goes to the cops?" He did not sound particularly worried.

Ricci showed his teeth in an unhumorous grin. "She won't go for no cops. That kid reckons she's smart, and maybe she is—too smart for you leastways." He swung the ice round in his glass and finished the drink at a swallow. "You don't think good, 'Berto, you get excited. That's why you croaked the little guy. Polly's going to get mad about that, but the kid won't run for no cops. She'll go for that Limey godalmighty on the island to see what she gets out of it, and that means she heads for the waterfront. So let's go. Work separate. Check down every street toward the boats and then meet up at that Palazzo place."

"Only I'd had a gun," Alberto said.

If possible Ricci's grin was even more mirthless. "There's aplenty of good canals around. I said let's go!"

Ricci was right so far. Angela was thinking of d'Espinal but she was making for a church at the end of the Merceria. Someone must call the police, she thought—because it was not right for Signor Cavalli to be left like that—but not herself. Signor d'Espinal was the best person, one could even imagine them being polite to him, and also there was the five thousand lire when she explained that now only she alone knew where to find the stone baby. But first there were far more important authorities even than the police to speak to about Signor Cavalli. Certain correct and proper things always had to be done for dead persons, and there was nobody here to do them for him except herself.

When she reached the Merceria, the most crowded street in Venice, brilliant with multicolored lights, windows of silks and shining glass, jewelry and flowers, Ricci was dangerously close. He had picked her up almost at once, but where he had to thrust his way into the river of drifting, chattering people, she seemed to slip through like an eel. An elderly, cursing porter blocked the way with his hand truck, a party of Japanese tourists marched with irresistible determination behind their guide, a harassed nun vainly tried to marshal what seemed to be scores of shrill, excited girls. And when at last Ricci broke through, sweating and cursing himself, Angela had vanished again. He passed the church, but it did not occur to him to look inside.

There was a service going on in one of the side chapels, and Angela made a little bob towards the lights and voices and the drifting mist of incense, and then took out her precious store of lire. This was really very difficult. Fifty seemed a paltry sum to offer for Signor Cavalli's soul, but on the other hand a hundred was rather a lot, especially since she would have to buy something to eat soon. Nevertheless she chose the newest one-hundred piece she had, dropped it in the box and selected and lit a candle. Then she made a careful little prayer explaining where Signor Cavalli was, asking to be forgiven for not doing more for him herself because she had quite serious problems of her own, and promising she would arrange for someone to go along to the apartment soon to lay him on his bed properly.

That was the best she could do, but if what Signor d'Espinal had said was true—that in Heaven a candle from a child is more effective than the blessing of a bishop—it was quite a lot. Next she must telephone the signore to explain what had happened, perhaps even tell him where the stone baby was if she could make a good bargain, and the best place for that was from the café-bar where she sometimes worked. It was almost all the way back to the Rialto, and she sighed gently and set out again. She emerged into the Merceria barely ten paces behind Emilia, going the other way.

D'Espinal too was telephoning from the hot, steamy atmosphere of a bar, watching the street beyond the open doorway. Paolo's voice was faintly amused. "A haunted graveyard? My dear boy, the whole of Venice is haunted. One would imagine San Michele cemetery less so than most places." D'Espinal barked a question at him and he said, "You sound impatient. Annunzietta? Of course she knows everything, but she's out visiting at this moment. I'll ask her when she returns."

Mrs. Teestock took Angela's call. It was a poor line with so much noise in the background, a nervous, breathless voice speaking close to the receiver and asking, "Please, might one speak to Signor d'Espinal? It is really most important."

She stumbled slightly over the name and Mrs. Teestock recognized who it was at once—probably speaking from one of the public telephones in some bar or the other. Really an uncommonly forward child, she thought, but she answered encouragingly enough, "Signor d'Espinal is not here at present. Can I help you?"

"Oh dear . . ." Angela whispered. The dismay was unmistakable. Half drowned by the sudden hiss of what sounded like a coffee machine, she went on, "I wanted Signor d'Espinal most specially," and then added, "Please, Signorina Emilia then."

That was too much. One ought not to feel this way, but one did, and Mrs. Teestock was unreasonably annoyed that the child should ask for Emilia or Harcourt and so pointedly refuse to speak to herself. She said, "Angela Caterina, is that you? I must tell you, Angela Caterina, that you are a very naughty little girl. Both Signorina Pentecost and Signor d'Espinal are in Venice looking for you now and if—"

Angela did not stop to hear any more from the indignant voice at the other end. She whispered, "Oh, please, thank you. I'll find them, then." And the best place to do that, she told herself happily and quite logically, was near the ferry station at San Zaccaria, where most of the people with private boats always moored them. She could not know that, working out from the Campo Sant' Anna, Pietro had tied up theirs at the Rialto steps, less than a hundred yards from where she was now. She hung up and set off again, plodding doggedly away from it back towards San Zaccaria again, evading one, two, and then three pairs of *carabinieri* with an ease born of practice and natural caution.

Ricci and Alberto were already systematically patrolling there, one from the palace towards the air terminal, the other along the Riva Schiavoni. They were both quite patient. Each time they joined up they exchanged a few words and started back again. Neither Polliano, nor the stone baby, nor even the cops mattered so much now; finding that kid and settling with her came first.

D'Espinal, Emilia and Pietro were at the far end of Saint Mark's Square, looking down towards the floodlit brilliance of the cathedral arches and domes rising above the dark, drifting crowds, and Pietro said, "Signorina, signore, this is no good. We're going to have a rough run home if we don't go soon. And you'll never find that cunning little devil in this mob."

"I'm starting to feel you're right," d'Espinal admitted. "Very well, then. I'll try one more call to old Paolo and then we'll come back with you. We must leave it to the police."

Still carrying the sandals and her portrait, Emilia said, "No. Bring the boat round to San Zaccaria,

Pietro. We'll meet you there in half an hour. If you really must call Paolo again, Harry, I'll go back to the palace. I'll wait for you at the Zaccaria front."

Pietro looked at d'Espinal and shrugged imperceptibly. At least that gave him time for a glass of wine, and at this moment he was drier than any of them would be for much longer if they did not get out of here soon. And with unusual meekness d'Espinal agreed, "As you wish, my dear. But I intend to find out where this haunted graveyard is. If it exists at all."

Angela missed Pietro in dodging two more *carabinieri*, turning along another *calle* to avoid them, d'Espinal as he was at the telephone in Florian's, and Emilia under the other arcade on the far side of the square. She walked straight between Alberto and Ricci as she hurried down to the waterfront herself.

People were still strolling and gossiping here, watching the flashing spectacle of lights and boats, although some of them were already starting to look anxiously at the sky. A damp little breeze was getting up, ruffling the lagoon and sending sharp waves slapping fretfully at the steps, and she moved along faster examining the boats tossing at their moorings, hoping at least to see Pietro. More and more were leaving now, and if Signor d'Espinal did not come soon she would have to go herself. It was beginning to look as if she must sleep in the gardeners' hut again tonight.

Alberto was already waiting at the bridge when Ricci got back there, up a series of shallow risers so that the arch was six or eight feet above the level of the pavement. He muttered, "Okay, we got her." Besides

moving like a cat and sometimes looking like one, he
had eyes just as sharp, and he jerked a thumb out.
"See that hat? Down by the water. Acts like she's
checking over the boats."

Ricci grinned. He said, "It's for keeps this time.
But for God's sake take it easy, 'Berto. We got to head
her off into some dark street."

She reached the ferry station, and after one final
look back turned away disconsolately. The riva here
was a wide rectangle of pavement with the waterfront at one side, the Old Prison and the Danieli
Hotel facing it fifty yards away, and a canal cutting off
either end, each with its own bridge. Still without seeing Alberto and Ricci, Angela moved in towards the
bridge on her right, which she must cross before starting off for the Exposition Gardens and her hut. But
just at this end was a tight little laughing circle with
strange, shrill cries coming from somewhere inside it,
and she edged in curiously, although the first few
spots of rain were already falling. In the center was an
old man with a comic toy: a little yellow rubber
puppy struggling and sinking in a pail of water, making agonized drowning shrieks until it went down with
a last, despairing gurgle. Angela started to laugh too,
but then looked up and stopped with a painful gasp.
For a moment she felt like that poor, silly puppy herself. Alberto and Ricci were standing there watching
her and blocking her only way to the bridge.

Glancing at the other escape, a hundred yards left
to the next canal and its bridge over to the palace arcades, she began to push back, and at that moment
the rain swept down in sudden drifting sheets, turning

the overhead lamps into misty halos and the pavement into a splashing mirror scarred by reflections and black, racing shadows. The old man snatched up his miserable rubber puppy dogs, and the crowd melted as if it had been washed away, rushing like ants towards the shelter of the buildings. But Angela hesitated for just one second too long before starting that way too. Alberto and Ricci closed in on her, and with a single, half-choked scream she swung round and started to run wildly in the only direction she could go now—towards the ferry station.

They looked innocently like last passengers running for the boat waiting there, the man at the ticket gate bawling, "*Presto* now. We can't wait all night." Except to Emilia. Reaching the palace arcades only seconds before the rain came streaming in, she saw the crowd break and scatter, leaving only three black figures against a glittering curtain, and the color of Angela's hat under the lamps—even now she was still holding it onto her head. Emilia started out automatically, crying, "Angela!" but they were a hundred yards or more away, the other side of a wide canal and almost on the boat; there was no way of reaching them in time. Nevertheless she ran on until she realized it was futile, stopped and turned back for the arcades and the square to look for d'Espinal. With a curious sort of angry detachment she thought it was infuriating how instinctively one turned to that man.

Breathing an inarticulate prayer to Sant' Anna, Angela thrust a coin out and snatched at her ticket, while the ship's bell rang impatiently and a deckhand stood ready to close the rail. She raced across the floating pontoon and scrambled aboard, pausing only to glance back at Alberto and Ricci. The boat was already moving, the ticket man seemed to be arguing with them, and for one hopeful moment she thought they might be too late. But then they came hammering over the wet boards. The deckhand treacherously dragged them across the widening gap.

Blurred silvery through the rods of falling rain, the lights of Venice were swinging away, while Alberto and Ricci stood there looking down at her, and Angela stared back at them rigid with fright and defeat. She was not thinking very clearly, but she did realize that whatever happened she must not go near the rail, not with all that black water swirling past below; she must get up into the saloon, where there were more people than here on the deck. But before she could move, Ricci grinned at her painfully. He whispered, "You caused us a lot of trouble, kid."

"Please," Angela begged, "I haven't been to the police, and I won't go to them, I promise. And I really can tell you where the stone baby is. I really will."

Alberto fingered the long scratches on his cheek and shook his head slowly. "Like you said that before." He sounded almost reproachful.

Ricci stared at him. "Take it easy now, 'Berto. We still got problems." There seemed to be some kind of message passing between them, and Alberto glanced round at the few passengers on the wooden seats, watching them quietly and incuriously. They did not look as if they would do much to help her, Angela thought, and Ricci asked, "Why don't we go up into the saloon, give the kid some supper like we told her?"

"Oh yes, please," Angela said. There was still a chance, she told herself obstinately. Once let them get to the Lido and it was only a very short distance to her friend's café on the avenue. These men were not very clever, she had escaped them twice already and she could again.

They walked up the stairs to the saloon, one each side of her, and Ricci pushed open the glass doors. It was warm and bright and dry here, with a smell of coffee and wine, people round the bar laughing about the rain and shouting at each other cheerfully, and Angela felt a little more of her confidence returning, reminding herself that Sant' Anna had never failed her yet. Ricci pushed her down at a table in the corner, smiling at her. "You sit there, kid. 'Berto'll look after you. I'll get you something good."

Alberto was smiling too, and with a flash of defiance she told him, "I could ask someone to help me. And ride back to Venice on this ship."

"It's the last boat, kid. And who'd believe a little tramp like you?" he asked reasonably. "Look at yourself."

That was probably true, she thought sadly: bare feet and a torn shirt, her clothes sticking to her and her beautiful hat a sodden mass. She took it off to examine it and Ricci came back with a big steaming mug of coffee, making her realize how cold she was after being so hot all day. Cupping her hands, she drank it thirstily while they both watched her, and Ricci said, "Now, kid, you tell us then?"

172

Angela eyed them doubtfully. It was very hard to give up like this. "Signor d'Espinal would give me five thousand lire if I told him."

"Only five thousand?" Ricci asked. "It's not all that much. Mr. Polliano'd make it more than that. Ain't that so, 'Berto?"

"Sure he would," Alberto agreed tonelessly. "A lot more."

It took them just five minutes to get the story out of her, everything about Signor Cavalli and the stone baby, and at last, sitting opposite her, Ricci said, "An old graveyard, is it?" He looked up at Alberto and asked, "Ain't that kinda smart, 'Berto? An old graveyard where nobody ever goes. Couldn't be a better place to hide a baby. So you show us where it is?" She did not answer, and he repeated, "You show us where it is and maybe we forget all the trouble you caused us and scratching 'Berto's face and everything. Maybe we do something a lot better than five thousand lousy lire." He looked at Alberto again.

They might, she decided. At least if they got the baby they might let her go, and she had promised she would not tell the police. She looked through the window at the lights and the wet, deserted roadway of Santa Maria Elisabetta wheeling round towards them.

Pushing impatiently through the people under the arcades, finally splashing out into the open to move faster, Emilia ran up to the square. She met d'Espinal taking shelter near the Campanile and, with a sudden flare of confused feeling which surprised and shocked her, she thought furiously that she had never seen anyone so damnably self-assured—and she had never seen anyone she wanted more. He looked at her, faintly surprised, murmured, "My dear!" and then with his maddening, eternally amusing manner of arranging everything magnificently added, "At least we've solved one mystery: our haunted graveyard. Annunzietta knew, of course . . ."

She said, "Damn your haunted graveyard," and stopped. "I'm sorry, Harry. Harry, that child. She went on the Lido ferry. It's the last one. And those men followed her."

As they sometimes did, all of his grand poses dropped away suddenly. "I see. Then we must find Pietro—quickly."

Hours later, it seemed, though in fact barely twenty minutes, they were bumping and skidding across the water, Emilia crouching beside Pietro under the windshield and d'Espinal finding what shelter he could in the rear cockpit. It was inconceivable, he thought, that the lagoon could so quickly become such an infinity of malevolent darkness. Even when they reached the Lido, so long after the ferry, they did not know where to look. The police themselves, he suspected, were taking that view also, had said nearly as much on the telephone: they could find the child in time and in daylight, but at night and in this weather the chances were almost negligible. But there was still one possibility. Bracing himself against the lurching boat, he leaned forward and bawled in Pietro's ear, "Make for San Niccolò."

Emilia turned a white, blurred face to him, and he shouted, "Annunzietta. That's her haunted graveyard —an old forgotten Jewish cemetery on the San Niccolò road. That's where the child says Cavalli disappeared. I think he took the Cupid there and she knows. I think she might try to bargain with it." Emilia cried something back at him, lost in the rush of spray and wind and rain, and he said peevishly, "We've got to start somewhere."

Pietro nodded and the boat heeled over, the lights of Santa Elisabetta swinging abeam and becoming individual lamps streaming past. In one more minute they had passed the last of the buildings, closing the banks of trees, and he cut off the motor; they drifted on silently in darkness again, but the rain was easing and even a faint, pale haze of moonlight was starting to break through. Then he muttered, "Here," and the boat grounded softly. He passed out a heavy torch, produced a short boathook from somewhere grimly, and d'Espinal said, "My dear fellow, do be careful with that thing."

On the road it was very quiet, only the soft drip of water from the trees. There was no sign of movement, and Emilia whispered, "There's nothing here," but d'Espinal swung the torch experimentally. It picked up something lying in the grass, limp and sodden but still recognizable in its gaudy coloring. Emilia caught her breath harshly and started to run, and at the same time there was the sound of movement from somewhere ahead and a sudden cry.

D'Espinal was never to forget his first, startled impression when they found the gate: broken tombstones glistening wetly, a tangle of branches like angular snakes glittering with water drops, and two dark figures—white faces staring into the beam of light. They were backed up against what looked like an old wall; there was no sign of Angela, and Emilia blundered forward wildly, demanding, "Where is she?" Pietro growled, "Keep back, signorina," and hefted his boathook.

The big one seemed to be lifting something from a slab, dropping it again as they closed in, and the other turned on Emilia savagely. Roaring, "Would you, by God?" d'Espinal brought the torch down with a crash on Ricci's head; the thing splintered, but it stopped him for just long enough and, now beside himself with rage, d'Espinal planted an unscientific blow on his nose. The moonlight was strengthening, just enough to see Emilia searching for the girl, Pietro at the other fellow, and Ricci coming back with something glittering in his hand. D'Espinal felt the point of a knife tear at his sleeve, was even more outraged, and somehow hit him again.

It became a black confusion, slipping and thrashing in the mud and the clinging undergrowth, and d'Espinal knew suddenly that this small, evil brute was too fast and too murderous for him. Panting heavily, he dodged another thrust, tried blindly to get only one more blow in and stumbled to his knees. Swearing breathlessly, he twisted sideways to evade Ricci's arm sweeping down again, heard from somewhere a dull, hard crack and half glimpsed Alberto collapsing backwards. Then Pietro swept him aside unceremoniously. He saw the boathook swing up and fall, watched Ricci sway and slide down quite slowly with an astonishing look of sleepy incredulity on his face, while Pietro muttered, "Well, that settles it."

Except for the sound of Emilia moving through the

bushes, it was very quiet again. The moon was brighter, and without surprise d'Espinal found himself looking down at the Cupid: the faintly mischievous smile on its lips and now one leg broken off below the knee. For the present, at least, he was not particularly interested in it. Pietro himself was examining Ricci and Alberto with evident satisfaction, turning Ricci over and announcing comfortably, "Well, I haven't killed them, and that's a pity, though perhaps it's a good thing too, but they'll certainly sleep for quite a while yet. My God, what animals!"

At that moment Emilia called out sharply, and they stumbled round another sodden path to her. Angela was there, a small, crumpled figure sprawled against one of the tombstones, and Emilia was bending over the child with one arm round her shoulders. She said, "It's all right, I think. She's more dazed than hurt. I think she must have been trying to run away and just stumbled. But she's terribly wet and cold. Let's get out of this place, Harry."

"Let us indeed." He took her up easily, surprised and rather shocked to find how light she was. "And I hope these quiet old people sleeping here will forgive our unseemly intrusion. I think they will." He added over his shoulder, "Pietro, old friend, bring that troublesome Cupid, will you? All of it."

Back to the old manner already, Emilia thought rather sardonically—rain-soaked and muddied, one sleeve cut from elbow to cuff, carrying a half-conscious child in his arms, but back to the old manner. She asked, "Harry, why not leave it here? Hasn't it caused enough trouble?"

Even in the vague light she could see his wolfish expression. "We've more need of it than ever now, my dear. I am excessively annoyed, and we have a great deal to do yet. The first, to call the police from San Giorgio Piccolo and have them collect this precious pair. Shall we go?"

Chapter Ten

It was a busy night and morning. With the splendid common sense which so characterized her in times of crisis Judith Teestock announced, "At that age you can't kill them," and carried the child off to bed, where rather paradoxically, d'Espinal considered, Mrs. Pietro began promptly to fuss over her as if she were now a poor little injured angel. Then a long call to the Lido police, which in time brought a return message that the two men had indeed been picked up, and the puzzled, even somewhat plaintive, inquiry as to what had hit them. This was a little more difficult (it required a nice diplomacy), but again the grand manner and a few more well-selected names carried it off. And after that the most important part of the night's stratagem: two hours or so more in Emilia's studio working gently on the Cupid, and then writing a short letter dated rather curiously "October 28, 1926."

It was early morning when d'Espinal got to bed to snatch a few hours' sleep before the police descended on them officially—when again, already instructed over breakfast, Mrs. Teestock was magnificent. She declared that the child was as well as might be expected but almost certainly in some danger of pneumonia, and one could not possibly allow her to be questioned for the present. With the instinctive Italian love of children, particularly sick children, they accepted that courteously—as courteously as they accepted coffee and d'Espinal's explanation of some of the events and of finding Signor Cavalli's body when calling on him over a small business matter. They were puzzled—especially since so far Ricci and Alberto were also refusing to talk—and not entirely satisfied, but at last they left just as courteously, even hinting that they could not possibly imagine anything dubious about the signore, Signora Teestock or Isola San Giorgio Piccolo. Reflecting piously that perfect respectability has its own rewards, d'Espinal made one more telephone call.

Then he brought the Cupid down from the studio and arranged it carefully, with its broken leg, on the teak garden table on the patio, placed the original Sabbioni documents beside it and sat down patiently to wait. When Emilia and Mrs. Teestock came out they found him benevolently contemplating the sparkling, newly washed freshness of the garden, the placid blue silk of the lagoon and a taxi approaching with the sun glinting from its woodwork and chrome and glass. "So he is coming?" Emilia asked.

"He couldn't really do anything else," d'Espinal told her, and went across the grass to the old red-brick landing steps to watch the boat idling in, a solitary gray figure in the stern looking up at him. He said, "Good morning, Mr. Polliano. It's kind of you to come at such short notice."

Icarus Polliano climbed ashore carefully, complaining, "See here, I don't get it. I have a call from the *carabinieri* that my boys are in some hospital, but they won't let me go talk to them. They tell me to stick around too. And there's something about that

Cavalli. Seems he got beat up. And now this call from you. What in hell goes on?"

"A great deal, I fear." D'Espinal appeared to be studying the distant buildings of Venice gleaming softly across the water. "Signor Cavalli died somewhat unexpectedly last night. It appears also that a small girl happened to witness the unfortunate occurrence, or at least some part of it, and your men Riccardo Castello and Alberto Mazzoni later abducted this child, obviously with intent to silence her too."

Polliano's face closed into a sort of hard stillness while d'Espinal went on, "However, you'll be happy to hear that she is now quite safe with us, though a little shocked. We couldn't think of letting the police trouble her yet, of course, but children recover quickly. In a few days they'll be all agog to hear of her adventures."

"Why don't you talk straight?" Polliano asked.

"Why not indeed? Shall we go and sit down, and discuss more pleasant things? The Cupid perhaps. At least come and look at it."

He led him across to the patio, where Mrs. Teestock, rather like a matronly figure of Justice, inclined her head graciously and Emilia stood back in the window watching them—or watching d'Espinal. Dappled with broken sunlight through the vines, it lay there sleeping peacefully, the faint smile on its lips and its childish limbs relaxed, yet still looking as if a whisper might awaken it. Polliano stared down at it expressionlessly. He said, "Sure, it's pretty. But it's kinda small. And it's broken."

"So are many of the greatest works," d'Espinal observed. "The Venus of Milo, the Winged Victory of Samothrace. Any competent Roman craftsman can repair that for you in a few days. And its size is hardly relevant."

Polliano shook his head. "I'm not interested in it any more."

"Dear me," d'Espinal murmured. "After all our trouble? After everybody's trouble? That's hardly grateful, you know."

"Mr. Polliano," Emilia asked suddenly, "would you mind telling us: Why were you ever interested?"

He looked from her to Mrs. Teestock, who still seemed to exert some curious influence on him, d'Espinal thought. "It was a fancy I took," he muttered, and then demanded angrily, "Okay, so what's so nuts about that? Don't you ever start something, thinking it's easy, and then find other folks let you in for trouble?"

"All too often," Mrs. Teestock agreed feelingly.

He nodded. "So that's the way it is. I just wanted to buy a statue. I just wanted to present it to my hometown. And what's so wrong about that? Other folks do it. Far as I can make out, it's a regular thing. I'll tell you, ma'am, this place I come from, where I was a kid, is just the most damn awful lousy dump ever. I reckon that's why I lit off out of it. All the same it's my home, and I reckon to go back there in the end. So I get the idea one day while I'm looking at the Michelangelo statues in that Medici Chapel: why don't I get something good like this and have it set up?"

"As you observe," d'Espinal said, "people have done

the same thing all through the ages. From statues to churches and cathedrals. It's a way of buying absolution. You are a Renaissance character yourself, Mr. Polliano." He did not add that there were some very similar ugly villains about in those days too, and they often ended their lives with the same simple ambition.

Polliano looked at him suspiciously. "I still say you talk roundabout. All I wanted was to have it set up in my hometown, maybe with a little inscription saying 'Presented by Icarus Polliano of this place.' You'd think that was easy enough, and so it should have been until this little Cavalli starts playing me for a sucker. That got me annoyed. I could've said the hell with it all. I near enough did, but nobody ever rides me for a monkey. Where this kid comes in I don't know. Alberto got something about her. Why they beat up Cavalli so bad I don't know either. Seems he got 'em mad."

"It has been a mess of incompetence, intrigue and mistrust from the beginning. And regrettably I was brought in too late." D'Espinal closed his eyes and appeared to be contemplating the mess sadly. "But fortunately I was brought in, and we can now perceive a more or less happy conclusion—except for Signor Bruno Cavalli. In consideration of the fact that the Cupid certainly is damaged, and in consideration of your own annoyances in the matter, Mr. Polliano, the price is now three hundred thousand dollars."

Polliano glowered at him. "You're nuts. I told you. I ain't interested any more."

Still with his eyes closed, d'Espinal asked, "Mr.

Polliano, did you ever hear the quotation 'Whoso shall offend one of these little ones which believe in me, it were better for him that a millstone were hanged about his neck'?" Emilia looked at him curiously, smiling faintly, and he said, "Come now, Mr. Polliano, we're in no mood for bargaining. The child can depose that on Tuesday afternoon, on the San Niccolò road, you deliberately tried to kill her. And I imagine that in the light of subsequent events the police will be inclined to accept that. We ourselves can depose that in our hearing you issued what could be construed as threats against Signor Cavalli. And we shall. The obvious inference will be that Riccardo Castello and Alberto Mazzoni were acting throughout on your instructions. In short, sir, you could be under arrest yourself within a few hours."

He did not answer, and Judith Teestock made what d'Espinal always afterwards considered was one of her greatest contributions. She announced, "In fact, Mr. Polliano, it would probably be the best possible thing for you in your condition—gastric ulcers, I imagine. A long restful stay in a prison hospital would do you all the good in the world. I understand that in Italy they are spartan but humane."

"I take it that your men will observe some loyalty?" d'Espinal asked.

"So long as it pays them. They won't talk until they got a mouthpiece, if that's what you mean. My lawyer's flying up from Rome right now."

"Then I suggest you see that it does pay. Bruno Cavalli died of heart failure, I understand—though he was beaten, of course. I suggest you have your lawyer advise them that being justifiably annoyed by your being taken for a monkey, as you so delicately express it, your men called on Cavalli to remonstrate with him of their own volition and became a little overzealous."

"Goddamn it," Polliano exploded, "that's the truth anyway!"

D'Espinal seemed to be in a mood for quotations. He murmured, " 'What is truth? said jesting Pilate, and would not stay for an answer,' " and finished, "There you have it, Mr. Polliano. There is no need for you to become implicated, but you could be easily— and fatally." He leaned forward to take up the bulky envelope of Sabbioni's documents, studied the Cupid for a moment through half-closed eyes and said, "In consideration of the sum of three hundred thousand dollars a small work in marble known as the Sleeping Cupid and attributed to Michelangelo Buonarroti, with attestations and provenance to that effect by Niccolò Sabbioni. The Cupid and its documents to remain in possession of Mrs. Judith Teestock until your draft is cleared. And that draft made out to Colonel Mark Raven, of Sixty-four Calle Della Pietà, Venice."

Polliano glowered at him again. "Another one?" he demanded. "God's sake, it seems there's fresh folks coming into this all the time. I never heard of him before. Who is he?"

"Colonel Raven," d'Espinal explained deliberately, "is the principal. He is the present owner of the Cupid. It was Colonel Raven, in short, who started this whole affair." He glanced across at Emilia and said, "I am merely finishing it for him."

Colonel Raven looked down at the slip of paper on his desk and asked, "Three hundred thousand? Is that all? You've made a worse mess than Cavalli."

D'Espinal sighed faintly. The fellow was addressing him as an employee again; it was really very foolish of him. But one could endure it for a few more minutes. It was even mildly entertaining. "A modest return on your original investment," he suggested. "Three hundred pounds to old Domenico Galli." He leaned back in his chair watching the jolly, happy little water ripples now starting to dance down the walls at this hour of the late afternoon. "I make it a capital gain of some four hundred percent, really very reasonable. Of course it will be rather less then that when you have settled the various incidental expenses I shall suggest. Very much less."

"What d'you mean?" Raven asked sharply. "Your own commission?"

D'Espinal looked at him wickedly for a moment. "I have rather different plans. But first let me summarize your position." He placed his fingertips together and gazed at Raven over them. "Really, the deceit and chicanery sometimes to be found in the world of fine art appalls me. As I have already explained, Sabbioni arranged for you to find that Cupid—which I can prove had been his property since about 1926—as he arranged for those jolly country fellows to come to you with their mysterious hints of a beautiful child lying neglected and forgotten on a remote farm. He already had a purchaser for it in Icarus Polliano, but he knew perfectly well that to sell such a person a worthless forgery could be an extremely hazardous proceeding. Therefore he needed what I believe is known as a front man; and you were ready to hand. I would say also that he already had the documents of attestation and provenance ready, including that delightful letter of the old priest, before even you 'found' our pretty baby. What an incredible old rogue —at that age."

The colonel turned on his bleak smile. "Let's just say it's a good story but it doesn't matter much." He flicked Polliano's draft with his finger. "That's the main thing. Not as much as I'd hoped for, but at least Cavalli's not here to claim his share."

"That is perhaps a fortunate circumstance, though Cavalli himself might have disagreed." D'Espinal looked at him thoughtfully from under his eyelids. "There is still a little more to arrange."

"Is there? I don't see what."

"I am referring to your own somewhat precarious position. Tell me, Colonel Raven. How minutely did you ever examine the Cupid?"

"That depends on what you mean by minutely. And what is my own precarious position?"

"Minutely enough to discover under the left heel two very small letters. The initials A.D.?"

"I did not," the colonel said shortly. "What are you getting at now?"

"Sculptors," d'Espinal told him, "rarely sign their work. In this case Alceo Dossena did. I've already told you something about that curious man." Raven made an impatient movement, and he went on, "I fancy that about the time Dossena made this Cupid in 1926 he was beginning to hear something of the very high prices his work was fetching and he took his own pre-cautions, by incising those two letters. They probably account for the fact that Sabbioni never attempted to sell the Cupid before."

It was an elegant little touch, d'Espinal considered, and he knew the initials were there since he had cut and aged them with extreme care himself; they would suffice for Polliano and this somewhat innocent colonel. He passed over a single sheet of paper and said, "The date is significant: October 28, 1926. We can ignore the flowery address to Anna, whoever she might have been. But you will notice the relevant phrase. 'Finished the baby yesterday, a pretty thing. This time if they think they're going to sell it for millions and give me fleabites, they'll get their surprise. I put my mark on it.' "

"That was not written in 1926." Raven's voice was contemptuous. "The ink's quite fresh. It's modern paper."

"My dear sir, of course it is. I wrote it myself. The result, as it were, of a little research in Rome. But if necessary the real letter can be produced in a few days." As indeed it could, d'Espinal reflected complacently. One knew a clever old fellow who could produce that or any other letter in a few hours, and on the appropriate paper.

Raven flicked it back across the desk at him. He asked harshly, "Will you come to the point?"

"With pleasure. Simply that I fear if Polliano's attention were drawn to those initials and this note, together with all the other relevant evidence, he would automatically assume the worst. He appears to be that kind of man. It is true that he has lost his two henchmen, probably for many years to come. But I imagine he would have no difficulty in finding some other person or persons willing to undertake a small private commission for him. There are some very dubious characters about, you know."

The colonel asked softly, "Are you threatening me?"

"Threatening you?" D'Espinal's eyes opened wide. "I'm merely pointing out your difficulty. And there is another yet. You do not appear to be very interested in Cavalli's death and the activities of this small girl Angela Caterina."

"I'm not."

"You should be. When Mazzoni and Castello come to trial there could be a great many questions asked about the Sleeping Cupid. The whole story might come out. It might turn a mere humdrum affair of assault and manslaughter into a national sensation. Another Dossena scandal fifty years after the first. And consider your own part in it. You pay a poor old working farmer three hundred pounds and you sell to a poor sick man for three hundred thousand dollars. It really wouldn't look nice. On the other hand, it is just possible that by a little careful diplomacy such questions might be softened or even obscured altogether. After all, the facts of Cavalli's death and the attempt on Angela Caterina are plain. The Cupid itself can have little effect on the verdict one way or the other. While the good Mrs. Teestock and her friend Mrs. Messina-Silvestro have a quite remarkable influence in certain quarters. But its use would depend entirely on their goodwill—and on mine."

He waited for Raven, sitting darkly against the glow from the window, but the colonel did not speak, and d'Espinal said, "Let us come to the real business. First, fifty thousand dollars to the dependents of Bruno Cavalli. Next, a trust fund of seventy-five thousand dollars to be set up in the name of Angela Caterina, the interest to be devoted to her education, general welfare and so on, and to be administered by Mrs. Judith Teestock. I may say that without that child both the Cupid and your own profit, what we shall leave you of it, might well have been lost forever. Then a second trust fund of one hundred thousand, this time set up in your own name if you wish, but again to be administered by Mrs. Teestock and any other persons she may nominate, for the relief of hardship and poverty in and around Venice. Finally twenty-five for me and twenty-five to Niccolò Sabbioni—I have a sneaking regard for the old rascal. You remain with twenty-five thousand yourself. Still a very fair return on your investment."

There was a long silence once more until Raven said, "I'll be damned if I do."

"You are more likely to be damned if you don't."

"D'you imagine you're Providence?" Raven asked.

"Not quite," D'Espinal peered down his nose coyly. "But it's not a bad part to play when He permits one to do so." He took up his briefcase. "Think it over, Colonel Raven. On one hand a quite enviable reputation in Venice. Mrs. Messina-Silvestro will certainly invite you to her monthly luncheon parties. On the other a world of trouble. I know which I should choose." He turned a look of quite imperial benevolence on the colonel and added, "There is one more small matter. You appear to have picked up some curious story concerning Miss Pentecost's work and myself. Exactly what it is or where you got it from I don't know. But I really wouldn't pursue it if I were you. One wouldn't like a lady to be threatened by another artistic scandal—and so unjustly."

D'Espinal was sitting on the edge of Angela Caterina's bed. He told her, "There will be enough to buy you a pair of new sandals, perhaps several pairs. It might even run to another hat and a dress or two. Colonel Raven is a very kind man."

"And five thousand lire," she said.

"You are a singularly mercenary little girl. Very well, and five thousand lire. But Aunt Judith Teestock and Signorina Pentecost must go to Chioggia tomorrow to ask about your family and make arrangements for you." The pale, solemn little face turned obstinate, but he held up his hand firmly. "We must do that. It is the law, and the law is something we are very careful about on Isola San Giorgio Piccolo. Moreover, I think you will find that a young lady with several pairs of new sandals, a new hat and new dresses will be treated very differently from a little girl selling picture postcards. That is all wrong and unfair no doubt, but it is the way the world goes and we must make the best of it. You will probably become quite intolerable."

When he went out to her, Emilia Pentecost was leaning on the seawall watching the lights of Venice now starting to glitter over the water in the short September dusk. Showing a hint of the slightly rueful amusement with which she so often regarded him these days, she asked, "And what now?"

"Now," he announced, "we must really look to our

own affairs. Notably, my dear, we must sell your delightful little Jacopo Bassano. I have intelligence of a fine, far-sighted fellow in the Middle East—enormously wealthy. He is proposing to set up a Middle Eastern Museum of Fine Arts to rival the New York Metropolitan Museum, the London National Gallery and the Alte Pinakothek in Munich. I feel it would be a Christian act to visit for a few weeks and give him the benefit of our help and advice."

Emilia appeared still to be watching the lights across the lagoon. She said softly, "Harry, I think you ought to know. If we're to go on like this you'll probably have to marry me in the end. Otherwise one day, eventually, I might be tempted to start another Dossena scandal myself."

"My dear," he protested. "You could never be so spiteful."

She laughed softly at the look on his face and slipped her hand through his arm. "That's the trouble. I'm afraid I couldn't. But you've been warned. Shall we go in?"